STEELMEN

BY JAMES LEES

All characters and events in this book are fictitious with the exception of some well-known, historical figures. Any resemblance to actual events, persons, living or dead is purely coincidental

STEELMEN

EPILOGUE

'Blast – furnacemen have always been easily distinguished by the peculiar red and scorched appearance of their faces. The intense heat to which they (blast – furnacemen) are exposed….creates in them a great thirst, and often a desire to quench it in something stronger than water.'

Andrew Miller 1864

HARRY BADNEWS

Harry couldn't quite remember. Couldn't quite place when drinking had become part of his daily routine. At first he was just one of those guys, out bingeing at the weekend, in the club or up the dancing. Then he'd noticed he'd started counting the days down in his head till it was time to have a drink again. Soon there were no days left to count! He remembered he'd switched to vodka from whisky a few years ago to hide the smell from her. She was always complaining about his drinking, fuckin moaning about it, implying he had a problem. Yet he'd always provided for her and the kids and he'd certainly never crossed the line with her had he? Sure there had been the odd blackout after a heavy session when he couldn't quite remember what had been said or done, but in 30 odd years he'd never so much as lifted a hand to her......well, just that one time.

He wasn't sure why he'd snapped that night but there had been something different about her, something in the way she had been flirting, a smugness about her that just fuckin annoyed him. She had been wearing that purple dress he liked but he'd been watching her cavorting with McSeveney, throwing her head back and laughing like a fuckin hyena. He saw her heading for the toilets and followed her, waiting outside for her. He couldn't remember what had been said but it seemed to him that there was something different about the way she was looking at him. A smugness almost an arrogance, yes that was it. Maybe, subconsciously, he really knew deep down what had been going on all along, but it would be a few years later before he discovered the truth, that they'd been having an affair the whole time. But that night, it was the smug look on her face that did it. He slapped her hard across the cheek. Instantly her skin glowed crimson, you could almost see Harry's handprint forming on her cheek. Immediately, he knew he'd done wrong, wanted to make it right.....but the smug look had gone, replaced by shock and no mistake. She had left him that time, just for a few days and gone to her sister Jean's. When she came back he made a fuss over her, even cutting back on the drink for a bit, but something had broken between them that night and it would remain broken but unsaid. Two years later she left him again. The drink got the blame this time but she'd be back in a few days, or so he thought. She'd miss the home comforts. The big telly he'd bought out of Dixons, the sofa with the big cushions that she had wanted that had cost nearly a fuckin months' pay! She'd miss the dug! But she didn't come back this time and now Harry was alone with no need to hide his demons and back on the whisky.

As he stared into the pollock (rail driven ladle like container) rapidly filling with slag metal he thought about the dram waiting for him at home. He felt the anger and bitterness rise within him as he thought of his nemesis Mc Seveney. He tightened his fist and gritted his teeth and spat venomously into the pollock below feeling the heat from the molten slag sting his face momentarily before the brief moment of inner rage subsided and his thoughts returned to the dram. Harry absent mindedly ran his fingers through a mop of thick, wavy and rapidly greying hair, the thick sideburns remnants of a bygone age when he strutted his stuff around the dance halls of Lanarkshire in his 'Teddy boy' days. You needed a wee half to wind down after the nightshift, just the one mind. More than that was the stuff of alkies and no matter what she thought, he was no alkie! Harry's job was as 'slagger' on No. 3 blast furnace in the giant, sprawling, hulking mass that was Ravenscraig Steelworks or 'the Craig' as everyone and their Granny called it. When the furnace was tapped for iron, slag would form on top and when the iron runner reached a certain level a channel known as the pye track would be opened by Harry to drain off the slag and ensure only pure iron was drained at the other side. This was done by Harry, at the right time, smashing a dam of sand built by himself at the entrance of the pye track with a long metal pole. Given that the temperature of the molten metal was generally around 1500 degrees it was fair to say that this work was hot, dirty and downright dangerous at times.

Harry rolled some more Golden Virginia from his tobacco tin and glanced at his watch a wave of dread suddenly washing over him. He could feel that knot in his stomach returning and tightening a notch. What the fuck was that and why wouldn't it go away? He realised with dismay that his neighbour today, or neebur as the lads called it, was young Jack Leonard. Jack was a likeable kid……for a Tim (Celtic supporter) anyway. He and his pal wee Ricky were as thick as thieves together but at least wee Ricky was a good Rangers man thought Harry. The pair of them were always up to something. Always plotting, always on the wind up, out on the lash, out riding wee cows. Cheeky wee fuckers the pair of them and no mistake thought Harry as he flicked the lid on his zippo lighter, catching a faint whiff of petrol as he sparked another roll-up into life.

The lads on the shifts worked to the continental shift pattern. This week for the lads on shift no 2, that meant dayshift Monday to Thursday, off Friday, then nightshift Saturday till Tuesday off Wednesday and Thursday (the Irish weekend they called it). Then it was backshift Friday till Monday, off Tuesday then the dreaded 5 shifter (dayshift)…..Wednesday through till Sunday, off on the Monday. Nightshift Tuesday through till Friday then the weekend off and so the twelve week cycle continued until you hit that glorious 'long weekend' when you finished dayshift on the Friday and weren't back till the nightshift kicked in on a Monday night.

The continental shift pattern played havoc with your body clock as well as impacting on your social and family life but the men did their best to make the best use of any free time. Playing nine holes of golf off the nightshift was a good way to blow off the cobwebs and get some fresh air into your lungs after a night of sucking up dust and fumes and you could still be home in time for the school run. The backshift would allow you some quality time in the morning and there was still time to get home and read the kids a bedtime story at night or for the young singles to head out afterwards for a night on the town. The dayshift had its faults, the scraping the car on frosty mornings, having to deal with the 9/5 management brigade or for the younger lads, trying to train yourself to go home early enough so that you weren't staring into a ladle in the morning swallowing down the urge to throw up after a night on the tiles. For all that though, it had its compensations, watching the sun come up on a new dawn and the early finish left you with the rest of the day to yourself. On every shift there were early birds and night owls but it's doubtful if any of the lads were able to train their body clocks to each change in shift pattern seamlessly. No, the continental shift pattern was a fucker of an existence but everyone to a man tried to make the best of it.

Mon	Tue	Wed	Thu	Fri	Sat	Sun	Mon	Tue	Wed	Thu	Fri	Sat	Sun
D/S	D/S	D/S	D/S	OFF	N/S	N/S	N/S	N/S	OFF	OFF	B/S	B/S	B/S

Mon	Tue	Wed	Thu	Fri	Sat	Sun	Mon	Tue	Wed	Thu	Fri	Sat	Sun
B/S	OFF	D/S	D/S	D/S	D/S	D/S	OFF	N/S	N/S	N/S	N/S	OFF	OFF

Mon	Tue	Wed	Thu	Fri	Sat	Sun	Mon	Tue	Wed	Thu	Fri	Sat
B/S	B/S	B/S	B/S	OFF	D/S	D/S	D/S	D/S	OFF	OFF	N/S	N/S

Mon	Tue	Wed	Thu	Fri	Sat	Sun	Mon	Tue	Wed	Thu	Fri	Sat
N/S	OFF	B/S	B/S	B/S	B/S	B/S	OFF	D/S	D/S	D/S	D/S	OFF

Mon	Tue	Wed	Thu	Fri	Sat	Sun	Mon	Tue	Wed	Thu	Fri	Sat
N/S	N/S	N/S	N/S	OFF	B/S	B/S	B/S	B/S	OFF	OFF	D/S	D/S

Mon	Tue	Wed	Thu	Fri	Sat	Sun	Mon	Tue	Wed	Thu	Fri	Sat
D/S	OFF	N/S	N/S	N/S	N/S	N/S	OFF	B/S	B/S	B/S	B/S	OFF

D/S – Dayshift   B/S – Backshift   N/S - Nightshift

Every 8 weeks because of the toll these shifts would take you were granted 3 accumulated rest days or ARD's. Often the guys with families or the overtime junkies would work these for time and a half, but if you took them off it amounted to at least a 4 or 5 day break. The dayshift was 6 am-1 pm, the backshift was 1pm-9 pm and the nightshift 9pm -6am. If you had a designated job and weren't one of the spare men, unassigned, you had to be relieved by your neighbour or 'neebur' and if your neebur was late you had to wait until he arrived or worse still if your they didn't show up someone would have to lie on a doubler (double shift). A good neebur would generally be in early to let you away. Most of the guys would try to be in for quarter to the hour and some really good neeburs would come in even earlier, especially on a Friday or Saturday when everyone wanted away sharp. Young Jack Leonard did not have a reputation as a good neebur. Generally he was okay on the backshift or nightshift (although he had even managed to sleep in for a couple of backshifts!) On the dayshift however he was an unpredictable nightmare and Harry dreaded the early morning lottery waiting to see if his colleague was going to trap. Wee Ricky was better, he was more reliable, always in about quarter to. The only danger with Ricky was a Saturday dayshift. Most of his mates in Larky (Larkhall) worked straight Monday to Friday, so Friday was always the big night out and Ricky couldn't resist a night out with the lads, couldn't say no. But other than the odd Saturday morning lapse, he was a sound neebur. 'Why couldn't Jack be more like Ricky?' thought Harry. 'In saying that, what could that fucker possibly get up to on a Monday night?' he consoled himself, suddenly feeling more optimistic. 'Surely to fuck he'll make it in? A Tuesday dayshift for fuck sake!

Harry glanced at his watch again as he took another drag on his roll-up.........10 to 6. This wee fucker better no be late! He knew the rest of the lads on the shift called him Harry Badnews and once upon a time he would have given a shit, but not anymore. It hadn't always been that way, in times gone by he had used to enjoy regaling the young ones with all his great stories of growing up as a youngster in the 50's and 60's. He'd have them eating out the palm of his hand as he told of the days of getting the trams into town, strutting his stuff up the infamous Barrowland ballroom back in the days of Bible John, the Mods and the Teds, the razor gangs and the scrapes he got into. He would tell them of going hunting and fishing down the Clyde Valley for your dinner, living off the land, of the time he and his mates broke into a distillery up in the Highlands, the time he got lifted for chucking a traffic cone at the cops and they left him all weekend in the unmanned jail in Stonehouse without food or water. How they had all laughed when he told them that when the cops finally arrived and discovered him on the Monday morning he'd said ' If yous had left me any longer I'd have been able to crawl between the fuckin bars maself!' But not anymore, he couldn't give a fuck for any of them them anymore, now he was Harry Badnews to all and sundry, a big fuckin black cloud of despair. To be fair, he'd had plenty of bad news to impart of late and no mistake. But fuck them, cheeky wee fuckers! Now where is this cunt???...........it's 5 to 6! Harry felt the knot in his stomach tighten another notch making him hunch over a little, the deep crevices in his forehead bunching together as he groaned the discomfort away. He was alerted to the slag pollock filling up by a toot from the pug driver. With that, he pulled down on the hydraulic lever and swung across the 'dodgy'. The dodgy in fact was a little bridge, that when swung into position would divert the flow of slag into the outer pollock when the inner one was full. Then the pug (small locomotive) driver would move the next empty pollok under the runner. Harry, when sure it was lined up would swing the dodgy back out and continue to fill the new pollock. Harry glanced at his watch again............6.00!

JACK

Some 5 or so miles away across the Clyde, Jack Leonard had stirred from his drunken slumber and was in full panic mode as he realised he was about to further embellish his reputation as a bad neebur! Jack had a system for the early rises the dayshifts demanded. The system in itself was flawless, Jack however was not. His alarm was set for 5.10 am. Jack had worked out that he could enjoy two sessions of snooze button bliss before getting up at 5.28. This allowed him time to have a quick wash, a cup of tea and be on his way in good time to be at his post in the furnace for 5.55 am. Sometimes he would even get up after one snooze button session allowing his neebur the unbridled joy of a smart wee finish with the early birds at quarter to! However, this morning things had not gone as planned and Jack finally focussed his eyes on the accusatory alarm clock at 5.55 am! 'Fuck sake…. bollocks…..cunt!' Profanities abounded as Jack leapt from bed at last. The icy morning air enveloped him like a frozen ghost chilling him to the bone. It would have to be a quick sploonge this morning. He gasped as the cold water hit his face and then set about brushing his teeth for all of 30 seconds. Fuck it that'll have to do! He pulled on his clothes as quickly as his semi drunken state would allow, pausing only to curse the chair leg he'd just stubbed his toe on. As he bounded downstairs Jack realised in horror that the temperature had fallen dramatically in the night and his worst fears were confirmed as he peeked from behind the kitchen blinds to see a solid looking sheet of ice blanketed across the windscreen of his Ford Capri 1.6 LS. 'Fuck sake!' Things were going to shit after a bad start here! Well there was no time for the niceties of scraping the windscreen, that bastard was getting a kettle of boiling water fucked over it and no mistake! Pretty soon Jack was on his way, weaving carefully through the icy streets. He glanced sideways at the empty kettle on the passenger seat. Fuck it, his maw would just need to boil a pot of water for the tea today!

Jack sighed involuntarily, a wave of dread sweeping over him as he realised his neebur today was Harry MacDonald or Harry Badnews as he was known. Harry fuckin Badnews man! That cunt was just a big fuckin, black cloud, raining fuckin misery everywhere he goes, thought Jack. He felt a tinge of regret as he remembered Harry hadn't always been like that, in fact he used to be a right good laugh. But lately? Man, it was misery after misery.' Ma wife's left me, ma dug's deid, ma motors fucked, I got done for drunk driving, ma sister's got cancer.' Cunt needs to gie his self a shake thought Jack. Need to concentrate now but. He knew he shouldn't have been driving after last nights shenanigans but there was nothing else for it now. He glanced at himself in the rear view mirror flicking his dirty blond hair to the side, the blood shot eyes a souvenir of last nights ill-advised and impromptu piss up. Up the Airbles Road, that's where the traffic cops would be. Lying in wait for the unsuspecting speeding driver or the poor cunt like himself, still half cut from the night before. The Capri groaned as it began to climb the hill but then roared into life as Jack came down the gears, his eyes darting to the sidestreets right and left in search of plod. But Jack was in luck, no traffic boys this morning. His thoughts turned to last night. How the fuck had that come about? He'd been out with Gerry Bonner off number 1 shift at Jilts Bar in Hamilton. It was alright for him, he had the week off, some horsey meeting……Cheltenham week was it? He couldn't remember. He couldn't understand all that fuss about the horse racing, all the gamblers, even his wee mate Ricky. They were all into it, daft cunts throwing good money after bad, after all when have you ever seen a poor bookie as the saying goes? Imagine taking a week off work for it! Fuck that, gimme the fitba any day! He had been full of good intentions, they had been out drinking since about 4 o'clock, Jack had timed it so that the racing would be just about finished. Jack hated the pub when the racing was on, he couldn't understand why they had to turn the volume all the way up to 90 deafening all and sundry when a race was on. Couldn't they just watch the fuckin thing? Anyway, Jack had been intent on heading home for about 7ish but Gerry coaxed him into a few halfs for the road. He came over with 2 Southern comforts to accompany the lager tops. He winced at the memory and felt the sickly sweet aftertaste in his mouth as he shifted his six foot frame in the low slung seat of the Capri. Southern Comfort? Didnae even like the fuckin stuff! Then, two wee honeys, just in from a day in town at the office came in and that was it. The wee yin wae the blond hair, pencil skirt and tight white blouse, ooft she wis tidy. He tried like a demon, his best patter, spent ages on her but she had a boyfriend! 'A Good Heart' by Fergal Sharkey had been playing on the jukebox and he tried to coax her onto the wee dancefloor. 'C'mon I've a good heart' he winced at the memory. 'Jesus, Jack' he thought. 'With shite patter like that it was no wonder the poor girl had bolted.' The girls left about 9 but the drink had taken hold of Jack by then and he wanted more. He couldn't remember the walk home but there must have been a fall or a bump, he felt a sharp pain in his right arm. Anyway, it was gone midnight by the time he finally staggered in the front door and now he had slept in. Fuck Gerry Bonner, his Southern Comforts and lemonades and his stupid fuckin horses!

Jack grimaced as he punched his card into the time clock. The digital display showed 6.14 am, it would be gone 20 past by the time he got down to the furnace. What a shirracking he would get from Harry Badnews and all the boys would be saying he was a bad neebur again, calling him a lazy cunt.........he hated that. But it would be alright, he'd work hard and make up for it, sweat that alcohol right out his system, make the old boys their tea and then go over to no.1 furnace and see wee Ricky to make plans for the rest of the week, maybe even have a game of cards with the squad. Harry Badnews was more relieved than angry when he saw the unmistakable figure of young Jack bounding across the gantry towards him. He had already checked the day book and knew there was no cover. He would have to work a double shift if Jack didn't show. With every passing minute Harry could feel his hopes of a wee dram slipping away, but, at last here he was. 'Fuckin time time d'you call this ya dick?' 'Sorry Harry' said Jack. 'That fuckin hoor ae a motor of mine disnae like the frost, had tae get ma Da to gie me a jump start. Ah hink the alternators fucked or summat' Jack lied. 'Aye right!' Harry responded catching a faint whiff of some kind of alcohol from the youngster that he couldn't quite place. But no matter now Harry was already walking away, heading for home and the dram. 'Next cast is at 20 past 7' Harry shouted back over his shoulder. Good, thought Jack, gives me time to get changed. His shift was about to begin, albeit a little later than planned!

After he'd gone into the bothy and got changed into his flame proof RFD suit Jack went to the mirror and made another attempt at smoothing over his mop of unruly dirty blond hair. He'd ditched the mullet look he had once sported a few months before starting in the steelworks after tiring of his Dad's jibes about looking like a big Jessie and it was now cut short at the sides and the back although he allowed it to grow a little longer on top. His Dad had also made it clear that the boys in the furnace would seize on the mullet look and any other perceived weak spot to give the new boy a bit of stick. It was this pearl of wisdom that had hit home and convinced him to make the change. Knowing what he knew of them now, he was glad he'd ditched the 'long haired lover from Liverpool' style, they'd given him enough stick over the hooped earring he had in his left ear, asking him if he was a gyppo or if he dressed up as a tranny at the weekend! In truth his hair styles had given much cause for debate at home down the years. Back in the early to mid-eighties he'd sported a Terry Hall inspired crew cut, rude boy look, too severe his Mum thought. Then, as times had changed instead of a trip to the barbers for a number one back and sides or flat top he had swapped for the salon and a wash and blow dry with a perm at the back or even streaks added for good measure. Footballers like Charlie Nicholas and Ally McCoist really had a lot to answer for! It had been a relief to all when he decided to simplify matters of his own volition just prior to his start in the furnace.

His tired looking, red rimmed blue eyes were beginning to slowly return to normal. Jack ripped the cellophane off a shiny new golden pack of Benson and Hedges and sparked one up and feeling ready to face his public now, he made his way into no 3 furnace control room. The control room was a myriad of gauges, charts and brightly coloured buttons and switches and after just a few years on the job Jack knew what each one of them was for. Despite the brightly lit façade like everywhere else in the furnace it was coated with layers of dust and grime. Jack, like Ricky was a 'G' man trained in all the different jobs in the furnace, there to cover staff absence or holidays and just generally go where needed. They all had different rates of pay, unused or spare 'G' man being the lowest and Stoveminder being the highest. Stoveminder was one of the most responsible jobs in the furnace and at no 3 that was the Chief's job. No one knew why they called him the Chief, maybe because he looked like a big white chief standing at 6 feet 4 inches tall with a white beard and hair to match, who knows. Jack didn't really like covering his job, maybe because on the first day of training he was told if he got it wrong he could blow up half of Motherwell! The only compensation of being on the stoves was that it was one of the few jobs where you weren't likely to get your hands dirty. Fortunately he'd only had to do the job on a couple of occasions and mercifully they had passed off uneventfully. Jack was quite happy covering as assistant slagger at no. 3 furnace and as luck would have it Ricky was covering the same job over at no 1 furnace, just a short two minute walk away, so they should both have some free time to catch up between casts.

As he entered the control room the Chief saw him glance at the empty chair where wee Rab McLuckie would normally be found. These two were a double act, like an old married couple. Papers out in the morning, first the Sporting Life then the Star to study the form. Like a couple of old maids they would bicker over who to bet for. Placepots, doubles, forecasts, tricasts, lucky 15's……..Jack hadn't a fuckin Scooby about any of it. Then out would come the crosswords, a wee warm up first with the Record then onto the holy grail, the cryptic crossword in the Herald. They got Jack into it eventually, chess as well and Jack would marvel at the genius of some of the clues the next day when they checked the answers. It wasn't often that they completed it but it was a cause for celebration on the rare occasions when they did. Jack always felt he was learning something from these two. He was honest enough to admit he hadn't paid enough attention at school and felt in some way he was plugging some of those gaps now. Jack glanced at the empty chair again. 'He's actually fuckin working, can you believe it?' boomed the Chief as if reading Jack's mind. Jack laughed, it was indeed odd to walk into the control room and see wee Rab McLuckie's chair empty. Jack listened to Chief's inane chat about his weekend building a swing in the garden for the grandkids and the fine Sunday dinner his missus had made for them all. 'Done us fuckin proud she did' lowering his booming voice in deference. Secretly, Jack quite liked to hear about Chief's hum drum mundane existence. It made his own seem so much more exciting and after all it was something he wanted for himself someday...... a pretty wife in the kitchen cooking up a storm whilst the kids play away happily in the garden. Jack liked the sound of that.........someday.

Suddenly Chief's tone changed and he leaned in conspiratorially. 'You hear aboot Tommy Wilson's wife?' 'No' replied Jack. 'Davie fuckin Kellacher's only bangin the arse off her!' 'Nooo' said Jack again, this time genuinely shocked. This was scandal of the highest fuckin order and Jack immediately felt bad for Tommy. He never did anything bad to anyone, one of the good guys, Motherwell fan too. 'You sure it's no a wind up?' Jack asked hopefully. 'Naw son, they were seen in the toon, in yon Italian on Bath Street. Bold as fuckin brass, sittin' right in the windae, holdin hands and snoggin the face aff each other!' 'Jesus,' said Jack. Davie Kellacher was a shift legend and no mistake, held in high regard especially amongst the younger ones. He was just a cool cat. Don't get me wrong he didn't like the fitba or the horses like the others but he had a presence, never stuck for words, a funny cunt but never insulted anyone. But it was his prowess with the women that was admired most, he could have any of them eating out his hand within minutes. A quick flick through of that floppy mane of jet black hair, a twinkle of those brown eyes, a quick witted line loaded with innuendo and a flash of his film star smile and he was in there, handsome bastard that he was. Jack had remembered how he'd pulled a nightshift with Davie last New Year and the lad had kept them all entertained with his great stories of gigging around Lanarkshire with the band he was in and all the scrapes he'd got into pursuing his favourite pastime, chasing the ladies. Jack remembered marvelling at him playing the guitar, fag in mouth singing the Streets of London or summat, voice like silk, he really was something else. Talented too. He was a fine artist and the bothy walls were covered with his witty cartoons and graffiti art. One thing was for sure, if Davie Kellacher was coming for your woman, you were in trouble, big trouble! At this point who should come into the control room but the bold Tommy himself, the unwitting cuckold, oblivious to his wife Angela's new favourite pastime. 'Morning lads, a wee bit rough there Jack son?' enquired Tommy ruffling Jack's hair as he winked in the direction of the Chief. Jack was in no mood for banter here given what he'd just been told, he needed out of there sharpish and had to resist the urge to give the poor bugger a hug! Chief wouldn't say anything but if he had a failing it was that he was the biggest gossip on the shift and Jack felt sure he would tell enough people for it to get around and then..............then they would all sit back and watch the fireworks. 'Aye no too bad Tommy, jist need a wee coffee to kickstart ma engines eh' Jack replied. 'Really? I heard it wis yer car engine ye couldnae get started' scoffed Tommy, but his banter was wasted on Jack, he had already bolted and was halfway out the door. 'Thank fuck I got out of dodge there', he thought to himself. He looked at his watch.........casting in 10 minutes, then all being well he'd head over to no 1 furnace and give wee Ricky the scandal!

Jack didn't get across to see Ricky as it turned out. Harry Badnews had left the pye track in a fuckin mess and it needed re-sanding. So for around half an hour Jack set about doing just that. The sand and the shovel felt heavy in his hand as he rearranged the fresh batch dumped by the digger machine. First he scooped out the excess both sides of the runner and then set about levelling the floor. When it looked right he began patting down the sides to form a perfect track for the slag to run down to the spout. Then, finally he would build the dam right next to the iron trough. This was the hottest part of the work and last night's cocktail of lager tops and Southern Comfort soon began to trickle down his face. He felt the blast of heat from the trough even with his visor down and then it began to steam up making it difficult to see. In exasperation he pulled the visor up to finish the job feeling the burn of the molten metal on his skin as he did, but at last it was complete as he squared the dam off at the top. He looked across with some satisfaction at his 20 meter long work of art but he was tired and hot after it. There was just time to drain some Irn Bru from his bottle in the fridge and maybe a quick game of cards before the next cast. The Chief's 'scandal' would keep for later!

THE SHIFTS AND THE OLD FIRM GAME

As far as Jack was concerned the only good thing about a week of dayshifts was the last one. Effectively after your 1 o'clock finish you had all the rest of that day to yourself and all the next day to play, with virtually all of the following day to recover before hitting a set of nightshifts. The best of all was the long weekend when you finished dayshift at around 1 pm on the Friday and weren't back till Monday's nightshift. This week Jack was off on the Friday and night shift on Saturday, normally this would have called for a big night out on the Friday but this weekend there was the small matter of an Old Firm game on the Saturday. Celtic v Rangers, a war of attrition that was about more than just football, a clash of cultures, values and of beliefs, full metal jacket required!

Jack liked his home comforts and he was well looked after by his Mum on the shifts. He had after all been her sole focus after his only sibling, elder sister Louise, had married young and flown the nest. She liked to make sure he had plenty to eat when he was around as she wasn't too sure how well he was looking after himself during the periods he would disappear for a day or two. On the backshift she'd be up to his room at 11 with the roll and square sausage or maybe a bit of French toast and a cup of tea. Then there were rolls or sandwiches for the shift ahead, lovingly tucked into a tupperware container and placed in the fridge. On the nightshift he was thoroughly spoiled, for his Mum didn't like him out working all night......young lad at his age should be out enjoying himself, plenty of time for nightshifts when he had a family of his own to keep. And so it went on..............a roll on something at 11 brought up to his room, then a cuppa about 3ish with maybe a caramel wafer or some digestives and butter. Dinner would be on the table for half 5 and the pieces for the night shift in the fridge ready to be collected on his way out the door. There was something of an unwritten understanding that Jack might fly off the radar so to speak, for a day or two on his dayshift week. Some lucky lady might have had the pleasure of his company for the night or more likely he had been out on the lash with a few mates and had crashed over at someone's flat or house. All that his Mum asked on these occasions was that he let her know that he wouldn't be home for dinner. On occasion, when Jack had fallen foul of this golden rule there had been words said and the phrase 'treating this house like a hotel' had been trotted out. Jack would fight his corner for a bit even though he knew he was in the wrong before finally accepting his reprimand. There would no shenanigans this weekend however, the Saturday night shift would see to that. He'd swithered over going out on the Friday night and maybe hitting some of the pubs in Hamilton before settling on a night in. He watched the Bill with his Mum. He'd always liked it and thought the storylines and characters were pretty true to life. After that it was the Equaliser with Edward Woodward playing a retired secret agent, now freelancing and looking after the 'little guy.' After scanning News at Ten for any stories that might impact the axe hovering over the 'Craig he decided to go to bed and try and get some sleep without turning tomorrow's game over in his mind. If he couldn't sleep he would turn the wee portable on in his room, maybe watch Sportsworld or something or listen to Billy Sloan on Radio Clyde. Billy always had the drop on the latest up and coming bands and anyway he found it easier to nod off with a bit of background noise. Tomorrow's game was a must win. For his team. Celtic had won the double last time out and on their centenary season too, what a year that had been but you could already sense the tide turning. Rangers had spent a lot of money bringing England internationals like Gary Stevens, Terry Butcher and Chris Woods in and were already 7 points clear in the league going into tomorrow's game. He tried to fight off visualising various scenarios that might occur during the match and shut his eyes in search of sleep.

Jack had started going to see the Celtic at Parkhead with his school mates in 2nd year, they would skip the train into Dalmarnock then walk round to the stadium and there'd be some kindly soul who would give them a lift over the turnstile and they would race into the colour and noise of Paradise for free. When they got too big for that you could crawl under some of the turnstiles at the Celtic end or take a runner at the ones at the Rangers end, jump up and holding onto the cage at either side force yourself over. Once, Jack had caught his trouser leg in the turnstile somehow and fallen over splitting his head open. The steward had called for the paramedics and everything but he was alright and they even let him into see the game. Then after the match it was back down to Dalmarnock, climb over the big red gate, along the wall......a 30 foot drop if you lost your balance, then drop down onto the staircase at the other side of the platform. Sometimes there were cops and ticket conductors on duty but most of the time they didn't give a fuck, they knew they were just kids trying to get to and from the game for free and couldn't be bothered with the hassle. Jack preferred getting the train to the match, liked the freedom and adventure of it but sometimes he got the supporters bus, The Manor Bar in Hamilton or The Commercial in Blantyre. He had gone through a phase when he went to a lot of away games but these days he was selective, just doing the ones he preferred. Dunfermline was a good day out, Hibs and Hearts away, a day out in the capital. It was the smaller venues he liked best though and the further away the better. He used to keenly anticipate the draw for the third round of the cup..............Forfar or Arbroath away from home was the sort of draw he hoped for. A wee trip away to somewhere oldie worldie and unfamiliar into quaint little football grounds where you could still virtually touch the players. Today he was on the Commercial bus though and would meet up with old school pals Mick Martin and Stephen Foley.

As it happened they were late getting away to the game. Father Dempsey was doing a christening or something over at St. Joe's and they had to wait for him.........couldn't go without Father. What if the hoops needed some divine intervention? The match was well underway by the time the lads pressed themselves through the turnstile and into the throng of the Celtic end and began to make the long trek around to the jungle. They would inevitably lose each other in the crowd but they would meet up again under the camera gantry.......under the feet of legends like Archie McPherson and Arthur Montford. Jack became aware of a roar from the Rangers end, the referee running towards the penalty area arm aloft. Shit! It was a penalty to Rangers. Jack couldn't watch as Walters stepped up but he didn't need to. The roar from the Rangers end and the seething mass of frantic, wild celebration was enough. Wee Ricky wasn't at the game Jack knew, but big DC Paterson from the highline off shift no. 2 would be in there somewhere celebrating wildly. Big DC never missed a Rangers game, home or away. In fact on the odd occasion he couldn't get his shift swapped he would throw a sickie so the gaffers all knew it was better to try and find someone to give him a swap rather than be a man down! Jack continued to inch his way around the ground, then just as he reached the edge of the jungle he turned his eye back to the play just in time to see the ball fly into the Rangers net. He felt the sway of the crowd push back against him, went with it and arched his back to stay afloat in a tide of green and white joy. But who had scored? An own goal was it? The confirmation came in the form of the chant from the jungle. 'Nice one Terry, nice one son. Nice one Terry lets have another one.' Rangers captain Terry Butcher had put through his own net! At last Jack reached his usual spot under the camera gantry and looked round for his friends. He was just about to put his hand on Stephens shoulder when his eye was drawn to the play again. The elegant Tommy Burns curled in a cross, the Rangers defence couldn't get it away then suddenly McGhee wheeled and sent a low shot into the corner of the net, 2-1! What a turnaround! Celtic were playing well, pressing Rangers back, whirling around like green and white dervishes, hemming them in and around their own penalty box. Jack caught sight of big Mick and for a few moments the three friends were reunited, then pandemonium ensued once again. A low cross in from the left and Stark was it? A volley through the defender and into the net.....3-1! The second half passed relatively uneventfully for an Old Firm game, sure there were a few anxious moments for Jack and his friends but Celtic's win was as deserved as it had been unexpected. Afterwards Jack walked smiling along the London Road, the police cordon down the middle between the two sets of fans. The usual insults were being exchanged………..fenian this, orange that and then he saw him. Big Derek Campbell Paterson striding towards him on the other side of the cordon. He saw his big shovel like hand raised across the cordon and for a second they reached out and high fived one another….a gesture of civility amongst a sea of animosity, then the moment was gone.

Normally after the game he would have joined the celebrations at the pub singing the Celtic anthems and the old Irish tunes, but he'd already had 2 or 3 pints more than he should have while they were waiting for Father, plus he had the nightshift to do. He didn't mind actually, the shift would be grand, he'd be able to chat to Ricky about the game, the big talking points, the referee, the goals, who had sung the loudest and of course he'd be able to give his Rangers supporting friend a gentle ribbing about the result.

Jack's gas was put at a peep the second he walked through the control room door. It turned out wee Ricky wouldn't be in for his shift tonight Chief informed him. His Mum had suffered a heart attack on Saturday morning and despite the best efforts of the paramedics and then hospital staff she hadn't made it. Jack knew his friend would take it bad, he was close to his Mum and his Stepdad Joe. Instantly all the excitement and joy of what he had witnessed just a few hours earlier was swept away and Jack felt only sadness for his good friend. Maybe later he would seek out big DC Paterson to talk about the game if he could be bothered, but big DC spent the night cleaning the sinter screens down below ground, wandering the belts of the highline for hours to avoid exactly that. Big DC liked young Jack, he was alright for a Tim but losing old firm games cut deep and he was in no mood for chatting with the youngster tonight.

A few days later Jack attended Ricky's Mum's funeral. Jack noticed that some of the spark had gone from his friend and hoped it wouldn't be too long before it returned. After the wake and the steak pie they had gone to the Butterburn Bar in Hamilton for a few pints. The Butterburn was a traditional drinking man's pub but well-kept enough to take your wife or girlfriend in for a drink with it's well polished oak bar with little brass hooks underneath to hang your jacket. Jack had wanted to bring up the holiday. It was normally at this time of year they would begin planning next year's summer adventure and this time there had been talk of doing something different from the norm. Maybe the Gambia or India or even Thailand instead of the usual offerings of Magaluf, Las Americas or Corfu. But it didn't feel right and Jack bit down the urge to bring it up. He would raise it another time when he could see the glint return to his friend's eye.

NO. 1 FURNACE IS SICK

A blast furnace is like a big giant soup pot, fill it with shite ingredients and sooner or later you'll produce shite soup. A crass analogy perhaps but it's pretty much what happened that winter. The powers that be, in a bid to cut costs had imported some new raw materials. Coal from Poland and the raw materials for sinter from China or some fucking where. You could see it was shite just by looking at it. The coke coming from the choke ovens had too much moisture and the sinter and ore were of poor quality, powdery and grainy in their constituency rather than the dry dusty lumps of greyish sinter they were used to. Pretty soon you could begin to see the effect of the new raw materials in the iron they spawned. Gone was the golden yellow vibrance of the iron and in its place a dull hew with a sickly orange glow at its edges and it trickled out of the furnace like a pensioner trying to squeeze the last dribble of pish into the toilet. The lads had to work hard, virtually forcing it down the runner with poles and rods into the ladles below. There was no doubt about it, number 1 furnace was sick!

As the quality of the iron produced began to plummet an emergency management meeting was called and a plan was put in place to nurse number 1 furnace back to good health. The men were asked to volunteer for 12 hour shifts for as long as it took, 24 hour cover 7 days a week. The furnace was to cast on the hour every hour, a relief crew on standby to effect any necessary repairs and spell anyone who needed a break. Basically they were going to cook up all the shite they'd filled it with then drain every last drop out whilst gently coaxing it back to life with healthier new input. Most of the guys volunteered, it was good overtime that was a given, but more than that, they all knew what was at stake. To lose a furnace and the cost involved, the lost productivity, it would be the death knell for the 'Craig for certain. Everyone knew the place was on borrowed time, heavy industry in Thatcher's Britain was a dirty phrase. Sure, the very first day Jack walked into the place the training officer had cheerfully told him 'Ye might get a full year oot it son, then ye'll qualify fur the full redundancy payment.' Yes, everyone knew that the axe was hanging over them and some day would surely fall, but it couldn't end like this, not because of some idiotic management fuck up! No, everyone would pull together and they would coax this fucker back into action and pretty soon they'd be making the high quality, award winning steel they were famed for. There had been rumours that one of the car manufacturing customers had told British Steel that if they shut Ravenscraig they would take their business elsewhere. All the lads knew though that when it came down it, none of that would matter, market forces would dictate and 'Black Bob Scholley ' the companies hatchet man in chief would bring down the final axe just as he'd been brought in to deliver. The finishing mill at Gartcosh had already been closed a few years earlier, the next expected move would be a reduction to a one furnace operation. When that happened the game was up, but not yet and not like this!

For days on end it was a hard slog, the iron continued to dribble out rather than flow, the runner and trough repairs were never ending with the constant casting and the stench of sulphur burned the lungs of the men on the deck. The weak chested and the asthmatics amongst the men were bent double trying to dredge up the rubbish from their lungs, spit it out, then big deep breaths and go again. Then there was the fatigue. Five and six days of this in a row had some of the men running on empty and that's when accidents can happen. During one repair to the iron 'dodgy' (a sort of hydraulic bridge designed to swing in and divert the flow of iron to an outside ladle whilst a new one was rolled into place on the inside track) Ricky had been spelling one of the guys on the beater. Basically when the iron dodgy needed repair they would strip all of the old lining materials out with jack hammers and pinch bars. It was hot and dirty work and heavy too as the dodgy was repacked with a mixture of a compound called ramtite and sand and clay. This mixture would then have to be beaten into place to form a perfect 'v' like channel with a solid clay spout using heavy vibrating plates and a hydraulic thumper like stick, called a beater. It was as Ricky had finished a spell on the beater he went to pass the heavy implement across to one of the lads that the power lever got stuck on the pocket of his RFD jacket and the weight began to drag him down off balance. Ricky looked in horror at the ladle full of molten metal below as he teetered on the edge and began to fall. Davie Kellacher saw it too and instinctively grabbed the collar of Ricky's jacket hauling him upright as the others jumped into the dodgy to help. The boy was chalk white, frozen with fear and the realisation he'd almost made a present of himself to a ladle full of molten metal. 'He's in shock, take him inside and get him some sweet tea and make sure he fuckin drinks it' said the foreman Joe, as they all contemplated what had just happened. Put simply Davie Kellacher had just saved Ricky's life but the pair never spoke of the moment again.

All of the lads had a healthy respect for the power of the blast furnace and the dangers it could pose, to do otherwise would have been foolhardy in the extreme. Jack could remember when he got his placement confirmed as the blast furnace his Dad trying to explain its make up to his Mum. 'A blast furnace is just like a time bomb, it can go off anytime'. His explanation didn't go any way to reassuring Jack's Mum that he'd in any way landed lucky but his father considered it good advice for the young man and what's more after spending just a few hours on the job so did Jack.

All of the lads on shift 2 had experienced a near miss or seen some sort of accident in their time although the overall safety record of the 'Craig had greatly improved in recent years. There was always some gallows humour attached to the talk of these near misses but accidents that had ended in fatalities were rarely discussed. That was an unwritten rule not just of the boys on shift 2 at the blast furnace but the length and breadth of Ravenscraig itself. Occasionally when a few drinks had been taken these events might be discussed in hushed tones. Like the time Ronnie Whelan had caught a blow out, a sort of mini explosion at number 1 furnace. Ronnie had never had a chance, there had been little warning and Ronnie was gone.........wrong place at the wrong time. For a long time all the lads had glanced nervously at the tuyeres (a tube injecting a hot blast into the furnace) as they walked round the deck after that but you couldn't live like that, in fear all the time and eventually through time things got back to normal. On another occasion three of the contractors went to clean the dustcatcher and caught some blast furnace gas......none of them made it out alive. Blast furnace gas was a killer, tasteless and odourless, the only warning you had if there was an escape was when your legs started to go or if you were lucky a sudden thumping sore head. If you didn't react quickly enough you were relying on a neighbour to pull you clear and if there was no neighbour you were fucked! One night, over a few pints in the Fir Park Club Ricky had told Jack about training in the Coke ovens when he had first started. All of the Ironworks apprentices trained in the various parts of the plant before getting their final placements. The By-Products plant was the worst and was just as bad as it sounded. It was generally cold, dirty work and you ended up stinking of fuckin Benzene all the time. The Coke or choke ovens as the boys called it were just as bad however. The ugly, space age airstream helmets did little to keep the coke dust at bay and the work was hot, dirty and downright dangerous. No, the furnace was for all its faults and dangers, was the place to be unless you were lucky enough to pull the white collar detail with the geeks in the technology department or in the stores. Whilst training on the ovens Rick had seen the accident that took the life of Benny Cleland, crushed to death by the coke pusher, pinned to the oven door after a safety switch had failed. Ricky had thought he was fine, he was talking away telling the lads not to look so worried, he would be having a few weeks on the panel for sure but he'd be alright. In reality it was only the pressure on his body keeping everything intact that was keeping him alive, as soon as that was released his insides collapsed in on him like a deck of cards and he died instantly. Rick could remember the white faced shock of the nurse trying to inject some morphine into him, her hands shaking like a fiddlers elbow. She knew what was about to unfold, that Benny was a gonner. Ricky had liked Benny a lot. He was one of the first to greet him when he started, always playing jokes on him, sending him to the stores for a 'long weight', taking the gammon out of his pieces and replacing it with paper towels, he'd ate the lot too, much to the amusement of the boys. He remembered his funeral at Airbles cemetery. His wife of just over a year weeping and wailing uncontrollably and the unborn son inside of her who would never meet his father. In truth that's why the fatalities were never spoken about. Not the fear it could happen to you or a desire to forget the lads involved. It was just too much to think of the families left behind and the lifetime of pain and anguish they would have to endure. No, the lads who went to work one day but never came back might rarely have been spoken of but they were never far from someone's thoughts and certainly never forgotten.

It had been a long hard slog breathing life back into number 1 but gradually a healthier glow returned to the iron and the instruments in the control room began to paint a healthier picture. The silicon content, always a crucial indicator began to fall within the acceptable range and the gas analysis was telling the technologists we were heading back to normality. It was a triumph of endeavour, of hard graft, a little bit of luck and good chemistry. After 12 days of round the clock care it was safe to say that number 1 furnace was saved. To the relief of everyone management announced a return to normality and the restoration of the normal shift pattern. During the intervening period two things of note had occurred. Due to the early retirement of one of the foremen, Charlie Gardiner, one of the lads had been stepped up from furnace 'keeper' the highest manual grade, to join the ranks of the gaffers. This had a knock on effect for everyone below and for the boys it meant that Harry Badnews had been co-opted onto shift number 2. This news was treated with disdain for the most part other than by wee Rab McLuckie the scale car driver. Wee Rab never had a bad word to say about anyone, always a smile on his face and always quick with a one liner to brighten your day. He didn't live too far from Harry and always seemed to bring the best out in him whenever he was around him. That at least would soften the blow for the boys from shift no 2. Wee Rab was one half of the double act of number 3 control room, the other half being the Chief. Yin and yang. Always huddled round the papers discussing the horses, putting the world to rights over a cup of tea with a dose of politics or current affairs or facing one another off over a game of chess. Wee Rab liked a gamble but both he and the Chief gambled pennies in comparison to some of the boys on the shift preferring to ensure that the household budget was never threatened by overly generous donations to the bookie. He was adored by young and old alike for his placid nature, his one liners and his hilarious antics when drunk. It didn't take wee Rab much to become inebriated. A few whiskies and a couple of half pints of heavy and he was up on his feet singing. 'Pennies from heaven',' the Green, Green Grass of Home' and the barmaid would likely get a rendition of 'You Great Big Beautiful Doll' if she was lucky. There were many great stories of wee Rab's antics..........the time that his long suffering wife Sandra came into the tap shop (pub) in Overton after his non-appearance with the roast dinner and plonked it down in front of him, removed the cloth on top of it and promptly tipped the lot over his head. Wee Rab just smiled sweetly at her 'thanks darlin' and proceeded to pass the roast totties around the boys in the pub. If his horses were running backwards, as they often were, he would take out his bookies line blow a raspberry at it and tear it into pieces before opening his arms wide and saying 'such is life'. On one occasion some of the lads had hit on the idea of a big day out and going to Aintree for the Grand National. A bus was booked and carry outs were bought and what a carry on ensued. Wee Rab, after tippling away at his whisky carry out was smashed before they got to Carlisle. At one point he had put on his jacket....'where you going Rab?' Ricky enquired. 'C'mon we're going to oor Sandra's fur a cuppa tea'. He didn't know whether it was New Year or New York! When they eventually reached Liverpool Jack and Ricky had set him across the back seat with a coat draped over him to let him sleep it off. A couple of hours later the boys went back to check on him and he was nowhere to be seen. In mild panic they headed back into the course to find him. One of the boys from the Clyde Alloy said they had seen him bouncing around in the middle of a Salvation Army brass band. Later when asked about this he merely smiled and said 'he'd been trying to attract attention to himself'. 'Jesus, what if he gets lifted?' thought the boys. Operation 'Find Rab' was stepped up a gear. Eventually they found him near Bechers Brook. The hood of his jacket had got caught in one of the fence posts and he'd been so drunk he'd been unable to free himself. 'Thank fuck yeez are here to save me!' he exclaimed as they untangled him. Ricky would later describe it as like a scene from the crucifixion as they set him free and he fell into their arms. Wee Rab was escorted back to the bus and never even saw a horse never mind a race that day.

THE KING LUD AND MEDIA STAR GUEST

Another consequence of the 12 day effort to save number 1 furnace was that most of the boys from shift 2 had missed their long weekend off. It would be a full 12 week cycle before it came around again, so that when it did all the lads were more than ready for it. A full shift day out was a rarity other than Christmas or the odd golf day out. However, after missing out and the exertions of saving number 1, all the lads were in the mood to cut loose and consequently in agreement that another such occasion was very much in order. As the first buds of spring began to bloom there would be a day out after the dayshift on the Friday of the next long weekend off. The starting point as ever would be the King Lud, Craigneuk.

Generally daytime sessions off a dayshift would begin just a short walk from the Craigneuk gates of Ravenscraig at either the King Lud or the Era bar. Jack preferred the smaller, more intimate Era bar, liked the pictures of the old boxers like Sonny Liston, Rocky Marciano and Jack Dempsey on the wall and the soft lilt of the Irish barmaid. The advantages that the Lud held were that it was a bigger bar and the lager was better, generally if you were a dark beer or Guiness drinker, the Era bar was thought to be better…simple rules to live your life by.

Jack couldn't resist a quick pint in the Era bar, a wee listen to Mary saying 'aaah to be sure, yer grand' when he offered for her to take a drink for herself on him. By the time he arrived in the Lud one of the tables was already engrossed in an excitable debate, no doubt about some horse or other. Normally Jack steered clear of this until the racing was finished for the day, usually just after 5pm, but his ears were alerted to the name Media Star Guest being mentioned. Jack cast his mind back some 11 months or so to when he'd first heard the name. He had been out for the afternoon with Ricky, one of the contractors Daniel Cotter, Gerry Bonner off number 3 shift and wee Rab McLuckie. The same excitable chatter was going on as today over the merits of this particular horse. Apparently Media Star Guest was the type of horse that performed when it felt like it, which wasn't that often. On more than one occasion it had simply refused to run, remaining in the stalls despite the best efforts of the jockey as the rest of the field took off. On another occasion it had been leading the field when it decided to veer off the track up the run off lane, fucking off in search of some bounty hidden to everyone else. However, when in the mood to race it was a match for anyone and young Ricky, as an avid follower of its exploits was convinced that day, 11 months ago, that Media Star Guest was going to race….. and win. What followed was quite simply one of the funniest things Jack had ever seen. In the end Ricky had convinced wee Rab to place a bet on it but no one else was having any of it and could not be convinced. As the stalls opened to start the race, the field bolted all except one. The television camera panned back briefly to Media Star Guest, motionless, unperturbed and staring blankly ahead as the jockey threw his hands up in the air in exasperation. Jack was already laughing by the time Ricky sprang to his feet and launched a tirade at the TV screen. 'Fuckin whip it, ride it ya useless baaastaaard! Look at it, fuckin look at it, the dippy bastard's laughing at me. See the day that baaastaaard dies am having a fucking party and it'll be fuckin corned beef all round. Aaaaaaarsehoooole!' The more Ricky laid into the horse, the jockey and the owner and anyone else he could think of the harder Jack laughed until he thought his sides would burst. Media Star Guest, the horse that does what it wants.

So here we were 11 months later and once again Ricky was convinced the horse would run this day. Jack edged over to the table as his curiosity peaked. 'I'll have some on that mate', he told Ricky. 'See, at least someone knows a good thing when they see it' Ricky exclaimed to the table slapping Jack on the back. Normally Jack would leave the placing of the bets to the others if he got involved at all, but today he decided to place the bet himself wondering how much to stake on this curious horse that did what it wanted and what the odds might be for an animal with a mind entirely of its own. He took the stake money and assorted betting slips off the others and made the short walk to the bookies. A glance at the screens told Jack that the fabled Media Star Guest was 9/1 today, the others had all bet on the favourite which was short odds at 5/4 on. Jack wondered whether to stake more than his usual fiver. He had owed his mate McGinnis a few quid from a night out the other week when he'd been skint and a wee win here would cover it. Three times he wrote out the betting slip then changed his mind, then just as he had settled on a stake £10 to win he heard the words 'they're off!'. Jack charged up to the counter with the slips in his hand but too late, the teller Pauline shook her head, 'Yer too late son'. Jack turned in horror towards the TV screen to see that Media Star Guest had indeed decided to run today and had charged up alongside the early pacesetter. Then after just 3 furlongs it raced into the lead and streaked 4, 5 and then 6 lengths clear, by the finish line the jockey was easing off as it won in a canter. This was a fuck up and no mistake and it was exclusively Jack's fuck up. Ricky had staked a tenner at 9/1 and would be sitting in the pub this very moment toasting a £100 winner! Jack trooped back to the pub unsure of the reaction he was about to get and nervously sparked up a Benson and Hedges as he contemplated his next move. He briefly debated just going to the bank and lifting his own cash to pay out but decided against it. No, honesty was the best policy here and besides he simply couldn't afford the loss on top of the money he already owed to McGinnis. When Jack arrived back at the pub there was much hilarity and back slapping going on as Ricky basked in the glory. Jack edged his way towards the table Ricky was at and with no little trepidation hauled out the unused betting slips and stake money. 'There he is!' exclaimed Ricky proudly, 'the only man with the gumption here to listen to me and get on board!' 'Errrm, I didn't get it on in time' Jack interrupted anxiously. 'Whit? How the fuck no, you were up there in plenty of time' replied Harry Badnews taking the words straight out of Ricky's mouth. For a split second Ricky thought Jack might be joking but a quick glance at the horrified look on his friend's face and scanning the pile of unused betting slips and stake money on the table told him otherwise. 'For fucks sake Jack!' Ricky shook his head a look of utter disgust on his face and stood up walking away from the table towards the bar. Still shaking his head Ricky said 'ma round as well, eh? Whit is it Charlie Brown always says eh? Why is everybody always pickin' on me?' The rest of the lads were delighted, after all they had all backed a loser but still they were all aghast at Jack's faux pas. Jack made his way to the bar and put his hand on Ricky's shoulder. 'I'm really sorry mate, I couldn't decide how much to put on it and then by the time I did it was off', he said by way of explanation. 'I'll go to the bank and lift the money myself, it's my fault you're no a hundred quid up'. Ricky turned and smiled at his friend and already his easy going demeanour had returned. 'Na, don't be daft bud, these things are sent tae try us, whit's fur ye'll no go by ye and all that. Anyway, I've a belter up ma sleeve for the next race, 12/1 shot as well, but fuck this fannying about wi' fivers here and tenners there, only maybe this time I'll put the bet on maself eh?' Rick winked at his friend as Jack glanced over his shoulder at the betting slip already written out on the bar….. £40 on the nose! 'Naw, please don't mate', said Jack. He'd seen this before when the horsey men had lost the first couple of races, chasing it they called it. Frustrated at losing bets they had expected to win they would pile on extra stake money in an attempt to get back ahead of the game. 'Mibbe its no your day mate?' Jack coaxed anxiously but he already knew his friends mind was set and he was fighting a losing battle. Ricky just turned and smiled at him, 'he who dares wins' he said quoting a Del boy phrase from Only Fools And Horses. 'If you don't want on this it's your loss bud, fuckin racing certainty' Ricky winked again and with that he was gone carrying the glasses back to the table.

Ricky went on to lose £250 that day and in doing so further enhanced his reputation as the unluckiest gambler on shift number 2. He didn't blame Jack and neither did the rest of the guys although it was the source of repeated hilarity throughout much of the rest of the day. All apart from one person that was………..Harry Badnews took every opportunity to raise the debacle with Jack and taunt him with it, to the extent that more than once Jack had to resist the urge to smash his fuckin face in. He never did lift his hands to Harry though because in his heart he knew that Harry was right and that he still felt the weight of the guilt of letting his friend down. As for Media Star Guest? It was entered in two more races that season and never set a fuckin hoof outside the stalls. Media Star Guest the horse that did what it wanted!

DAVIE KELLACHER GETS HIS COMEUPPANCE

Davie Kellacher didn't quite know why he was the way he was. On the rare occasions he allowed himself to think about it he soon dismissed any soul searching as a pointless waste of energy. His father had certainly had some influence on him for the short time he was around in his early years. Before he had reached 5 years old he was able to strum the guitar fairly well and was word perfect on the Mungo Jerry classic 'In the Summertime.' His father had also made him aware of the joys of the weed and the need to 'experiment' in life. But Davie Kellacher senior wasn't the settling down kind and one night he fucked off on the night bus to London and never came back. If truth be told, Davie junior's mother Anna wasn't too upset at his departure, certainly not as upset as someone hopelessly in love should be. She didn't really have room in her life for another man and from the moment Davie junior was born she was besotted and devoted to his every waking moment to the detriment of her relationship with his father. So much so that Davie was home schooled until he was 7 years old before the authorities intervened and threatened to take young master Kellacher into care. Not that being home schooled was in any way to young Davie's detriment. His mother taught him to read, write and count, encouraged his artistic tendencies towards drawing, painting and of course his music. She also taught him languages and by the time Davie started at school he could speak a smattering of French, Spanish and the Romani gypsy tongue that was part of his heritage. More than that though, she taught him how to treat women or rather how to please them and gain their trust. It was this skill that Davie used to greatest effect in his adult life.

At secondary school Davie proved to be a quiet but witty pupil, broadly popular amongst staff and his fellow students. He gained some early notoriety by resisting the physical intimidation of one of the school's erstwhile bullies and then disarming him with some barely disguised threats of retribution from the gypsy side of his family. Davie was selective in his efforts in his subjects though, excelling in the areas he enjoyed of music, art and craft technical but choosing to switch off in classes like maths and chemistry, which he'd chosen on a whim as Miss Watson the department head was tidy as fuck and had been the cause of many an evening wanking session. The formality of the exam process was an anathema to Davie and as a result he failed to even show up for most of them, even Spanish which he could have passed easily. When his school race was run excellent passes in Art, Music and Craft and Design were all he had to show the world for his time and trouble there. Upon leaving school Anna used some of his father's contacts in the local and travelling community to ease young Davie junior into the workplace and jobs in landscaping and out on the roads tarring the new motorway extension were found for him, but he didn't take to any of them preferring instead the party circuit gigging with the four piece band he had become part of, called appropriately enough 'Bad Risk.' Davie enjoyed the gigging life, getting the gear in the van and off to some new venue, a few drinks and a smoke before during and after the sound check. Then there was the buzz of the gig itself, hearing people sing along and getting them up to dance and of course there were always plenty of tidy women with interest in a handsome young man with a disarming smile and a guitar in his hand. One thing Davie didn't enjoy though was the constant bickering that went on within the band. Arguments over who was driving, who was pulling their weight with loading or unloading the gear, someone was out of time or the sound wasn't right and of course money. As talented a group as they were the chemistry between them was all wrong and it was never going to last long. When the opportunity to have a probationary stab at a full time job in the blast furnace in the 'Craig came along via a family friend, Davie was far from enthusiastic. However the gigs had dried up for the band and he needed to earn some cold hard cash, at least for now. So it was with no little reticence that Davie took his first steps through the Craigneuk gates into the sprawling mass that was Ravenscraig Steelworks one misty Monday morning.

To his surprise he found that he enjoyed his month's trial immensely. He was warmly welcomed for a start with no one seemingly interested in his background other than what team he supported and whether or not he had a bird. He enjoyed the stop/start nature of the work…..periods of hot, dusty intense graft followed by a chance to cool down and chill out with a smoke and game of cards with the lads. He particularly enjoyed the obvious camaraderie and easy going banter between the lads, something that he'd never really encountered previously. Before too long he had become Davie Kellacher, 'G' man on shift no 2 and what surprised him more than anything was that he was proud of the fact.

Davie was aware that his stock had fallen somewhat amongst the boys of shift no 2 lately and had some idea of why. He wasn't proud of his dalliance with Angela Wilson wife of Tommy the screen man on no 2 shift. He felt sure that somehow word of their affair had got out for although they had been careful perhaps of late they had taken more risks than they ought to have. Tommy himself didn't know, he was sure of that, there would have been fuckin murders by now if he had found out. However there was no mistaking the scowl on the Chief's face whenever Davie went into no 3 control room these days and even the easy going Rab McLuckie wasn't quite the same with him lately. He knew it was wrong what he was doing with Angela and that it would be dimly viewed. It was one of those golden rules to live your life by…….never cut another man's grass, especially not one of the good guys like Tommy. Yet he couldn't help himself. He'd first seen Angela when she came to pick Tommy up from one of the snooker days out at the Horse and Anchor in Cambusnethan. She'd had her hair scraped back, no makeup on and was wearing a strappy top and tracksuit trousers but there was no mistaking that hourglass figure underneath those casual clothes and the big soft brown eyes. Yes, Angela Wilson was a hottie alright and he'd caught her eye as well he'd noticed. There was a definite look over her shoulder and a smile that flashed in his direction, something to put in the bank for another time.

Another time came just a few months later when Davie ran into her on a night out with friends in the Electric Bar in Motherwell. She had come over to talk to him at the bar after smiling over a few minutes earlier. Her hair was down this time tumbling over her shoulders and she was wearing a floral dress of some sort of silky material. Underneath there it was again, that hourglass figure and that arse. Fuck! He couldn't resist resting his hand on it as she leaned into hear what he was saying over the racket of Taylor Dayne on the jukebox. It was then that it happened, as he tightened his grip on her arse ever so slightly she pushed right up against him rubbing herself against his rapidly stiffening cock. Davie knew right then and there that this one was going all the way and just over an hour later the pair of them were fucking frantically in the back of his Volkswagen Scirroco.

Angela Wilson had liked the cut of Davie Kellacher's gib from the moment she'd laid eyes on him. He was different from the other guys, self assured, interesting to talk to, funny and charming and devastatingly handsome as well. He knew his way around a woman's body as well. She'd came like a fucking train that night in the car and almost every single time since. He'd encouraged her to throw off her inhibitions too and they'd fucked on the deck of the disco boat the Tuxedo Princess and another time in the toilet of the train home from town. She'd take him anytime, anywhere, it was exciting and fun, a world away from Tommy's brutal weekly missionary position yawn-fest. Inevitably, she had developed deep feelings for him and wanted more but after two years of it Davie Kellacher was looking for the exit door.

Davie had tried to end it with Angela on more than one occasion but he found her charms almost irresistible and at times it seemed as though she had a sixth sense about when he was trying to pull the plug. On one occasion when he had been on an ARD (accumulated rest day) week off and he knew Tommy was backshift he had resolved to go round to the house with the aim of finishing with her. She had answered the door in the black basque he liked so much and stockings and suspenders and inevitably they ended up in bed as frantic as ever. Increasingly Davie had needed to talk her round as she began to expand on her fantasy of leaving Tommy for good. It had taken him hours one night, using all his powers of persuasion that it was a bad idea. He wasn't cut out to be a Dad, he told her, he was a serial failure in relationships, she was better off with the security blanket of Tommy, redundancy was coming soon, things would all look different then. Davie was now in near full panic mode whenever he allowed himself to think about it. No, this couldn't go on for much longer, there were kids involved. He wouldn't be the one to break up a family home and as for the boys on the shift? Why, he would be a complete and utter fuckin pariah. He was halfway there already with the Chief looking down his fuckin nose at him every other day. No, this had to end and soon. As luck would have it fate took a hand and something happened that very weekend to force the issue as Davie Kellacher lost his heart to a pretty girl in a cream dress at Hamilton Racecourse.

Davie Kellacher wasn't a great one for the gambling and failed to understand the joy that the many horsey men on the shift could get from handing over their hard earned cash to the bookie. He did however enjoy the casino and would on occasion go with Gus and Jake, his friends from the highline. He liked the pretty croupiers, the waitresses in their short skirts bringing your drink to the tables for you. He liked the easy going atmosphere of it all and the high class hookers with their long dresses on looking for an easy mark. Similarly, he liked a day at the races and would go to the Saints n Sinners meeting every year at Hamilton. Of course he would bet on a few horses but as usual his interests really lay elsewhere. He loved to see the ladies with their finery on, wide brimmed hats, high heels and flimsy dresses on, the guys all suited and booted. He liked the atmosphere as the well-heeled and well to do shouted their horses on over the line, glasses of champagne in hand. This particular day Davie only had eyes for one particular lady. As soon as he saw Lucy Angelis he was transfixed. He watched her for several minutes, her dress blowing in the breeze, the carefree manner of her as she laughed at someone's joke and absent mindedly tucked a stray strand of hair behind her ear. Simply put, she was the most wonderful woman he had ever set eyes on. Davie waited for his moment until she was briefly alone and walked across to make his bid for glory and like so many before her Lucy Angelis was soon powerless to resist his charm. Amidst the very first flush of their conversation Davie made a decision. He resolved to finally end his affair with Angela Wilson and did so that very weekend.

Davie and Angela had concocted a system to use if he ever needed to get in touch with Angela for whatever reason and wasn't sure if Tommy was around. Three rings on the phone, always from the same call box, then cut it dead. If the coast was clear and she was free to talk Angela would call him straight back. It wasn't a system they'd had to use too often as both Angela and Davie between them pretty much knew all Tommy's movements. Once Davie's hangover from the day out at the racing had subsided he made the call. Angela wasn't able to meet him that day and it was a relief to Davie to delay a conversation that he wasn't looking forward to having at all and by way of an added bonus he was now free to arrange a date with Lucy for that very night.

Instead Davie arranged to meet Angela at a café in Hamilton on Sunday afternoon, far enough away from prying eyes but public enough that she couldn't have a total fuckin meltdown or try and tempt him with her sexy wiles. Angela had a deep sense of foreboding after the call, fearing the worst. Why did he want to meet in a café in the middle of the day? He'd played it down, just meeting for a coffee and a chat, but Davie always wanted to meet in the pub or at his and the only time he felt the notion for chatting was usually in the aftermath of having fucked her brains out. No, something was up and Angela knew it.

As soon as Angela entered the café Davie spotted the worried look on her face. He felt sure that she knew what was coming but he determined to tell her the truth, it was the only way, even if he had to be brutal with it. He made the decision to instantly bin the 'it's not you, it's me' speech he had carefully rehearsed in his head that morning. No, the whole truth and nothing but the truth was the only thing that was going to cut the mustard today. Angela wasn't done up to the nines as normal. She had her hair scraped back from her face and was wearing a tracksuit top and tight denims. Davie figured that she had told Tommy she was going for a sunbed or some shite and had dressed for the part. As she sat down and they ordered coffees though, she unzipped the tracksuit top to reveal a very low cut strappy top that showcased her magnificent tits. Davie made a mental note to keep eye contact and ignore the sudden stirring in his loins. After some idle chit chat Angela pressed the issue. They weren't here for a catch up, what the fuck was Davie playing at? 'Why are we here, what's going on?' asked Angela. Davie gulped nervously, took a deep breath and then began to recount the story of his day at the races on Friday. If Davie thought that the mere mention of him falling for another woman would finally be enough to send Angela on her way he was wrong. She had questions, so many fuckin questions. What was Lucy like? How could he be sure she was the one, after all they'd only just met? Was she prettier, sexier than her? What was it that he liked so much about her? How had they first started to chat? What did they talk about? Was she a good kisser? Had he fucked her? Then the inevitable meltdown came and Davie shifted uneasily in his seat as the other patrons of the café began to glance over at the raised voices. How could he do this to her? They'd made plans to be together, she was ready to give up everything for him, Tommy, the house, the kids, everything. But Davie stood firm under the barrage. 'WE didn't make plans, YOU fuckin did! I never signed up for any of this. It was a bit of fun that's all.' Even at that, although Angela was broken to hear those words she made one final, desperate bid to keep him in her life. She reached under the table sliding her hand gently up the inside of his inner thigh. They could still be friends, they could still have some fun, his new girlfriend needn't ever know, she implored him looking deep into his eyes. Why put an end to something that had been so good for them both for so long? It was a last desperate act, a moment when Angela abandoned every ounce of self-respect she had in a bid to keep the flickering embers of her affair with

Davie alive somehow. Davie knew that this was the moment to finally cut the ties for good. He dismissed the images of the rampant fuck fests they'd had flickering through his subconscious and pushed Angela's hand away. No, they couldn't be friends any more, it was over. He stood up and with a barely audible 'I'm sorry, but this how it has to be' he made for the door. Before he stepped out into the sunlight he could hear Angela sobbing uncontrollably behind him. Within a few steps he realised he hadn't paid for the coffees, but he wasn't going back. It was just another thing to feel bad about. He didn't feel good about any of it. The affair behind Tommy's back, the lads on the shift looking differently at him and breaking Angela's heart all tore at him, but now at least he'd done what needed doing and could move on apace with the new love in his life, Lucy Angelis.

Billy Angelis had spotted Davie Kellacher for exactly what he was the moment he laid eyes on him……..a fuckin chancer. Normally he would have had someone have a word in his ear and get rid of the cunt pronto but today he was somewhat distracted with business matters and anyway he enjoyed the way the boy was making Lucy laugh. He just loved to see his only daughter happy and carefree, he would let this one play out for now. After all Billy was a respected member of the business community these days. Sure, he'd had to crack a few heads and grease a few palms in his time to get where he was but his days of intimidating ne'er do wells and dumping bodies in lonely nature spots were by with weren't they? Besides, there was plenty of hired help to deal with these matters for him now.

If Billy Angelis had known what was to unfold over the coming months he might have put business matters aside that day and dealt with what was in front of his nose, but he didn't and like so many before her Lucy fell for Davie's considerable charms, head over heels. Billy had underestimated this boy for sure, pretty soon he had Lucy eating out of his hand and it was to his great chagrin that they quickly announced their engagement after just 3 months of dating and Lucy's intention that they be married within the year. Billy began to wonder if he'd misjudged the boy. He was always charming and respectful with Lucy and the family and Billy's wife Margaret Ann wouldn't hear a word against him. There had even been talk of a job for the boy in Billy's organisation. The axe was hovering over the 'Craig and it was only a matter of time before it fell. Billy had a finger in a lot of pies and could use someone of the boys obvious charm and intellect. Deep down though, Billy knew that this boy had a monumental fuck up in him somewhere and when it came he would be ready to do what was needed. Of course Billy had looked into him, made enquiries so to speak. He knew that Davie was of part gypsy blood, worked in the blast furnace and had a reputation as a charming womaniser who smoked pot and played the guitar. His father was a waster who'd fucked off to London and the mother was a harmless pothead dreamer. There was nothing really there to endear him to Billy but not enough to condemn him either. This swarthy, gypsy fucker would remain on probation for the time being.

Davie Kellacher was in love. For a split second when he found out who Lucy's father was he'd considered cutting and running but he didn't, so enchanted was he by the girl. He'd stayed the course, played the game and kept his nose clean. He'd felt he was winning Billy Angelis over slowly but surely. Yes, there was still that hint of menace when he put his arm round his shoulder at family gatherings but much of the venom and underlying threat had gone from his voice and anyway Davie could understand any father wanting to protect his daughter from the likes of him. When the big day came Billy had done them proud. A country estate in Lanark was booked for the wedding and the great and the good of the business community and the sporting world were invited. Ally McCoist and Ian Durrant from Rangers were there, the McStay brothers from Celtic were invited but the club were apparently away on a pre-season tour so they couldn't attend. In a surprising hat tip to Davie's part gypsy heritage Billy had even booked a Spanish guitar band to play a short half hour set and they went down a storm. Davie didn't invite too many from the shift to the wedding, he couldn't risk the likes of wee Rab McCluckie embarrassing the fuckin life out of him with his antics. Then there was Tommy Wilson. Apparently Tommy was more than a little miffed he didn't warrant even a night time invitation but he couldn't have Angela there making eyes at him or worse getting blind drunk and blurting something out creating a scene. No, he played safe. The young lads Jack and Ricky were invited and arrived both with pretty young girls on their arm wearing short sexy dresses. Sure they would get drunk but they would help the party go with a swing and wouldn't let Davie down. Then, there were his mates Jake and Gus from the highline. They knew how to conduct themselves in such company and would do Davie proud. That was it, they were the only risks he would take with the boys from shift no 2. As it turned out he needn't have worried too much. Some of these clowns of 'businessmen' were even worse behaved than steelworkers!

Yes, married life was good for Davie Kellacher. The wedding and subsequent honeymoon in Jamaica had been a dream and then they'd come home to a fully furnished show home in Cambusnethan courtesy of one Billy Angelis. Just one thing was nagging away at Davie, gnawing away at his contentedness. He needed a wee blow out. He'd been good for so long. Hadn't even looked at another woman, hadn't touched a joint in months. Oh he was enjoying the life Billy Angelis had mapped out for him, the pantry full of fine wines, the surround sound stereo and the plush shag pile carpets. He just needed a wee blow out, just to get it out his system. A fishing weekend with Gus and Jake had been planned. The wee cabin near Loch Awe during a summer weekend. The place would be hoaching with tourists as well. No doubt some lucky American or Aussie girl would be on the receiving end of the famous Davie Kellacher charm. But that was months away, he was aching to cut loose a bit. So, it was with thinly disguised joy that Davie greeted the news that his pretty new bride was intent on visiting her best friend Dawn for the weekend down in London where she was at university. He did all he could to encourage this trip without over egging it and so it came that Lucy would visit Dawn over a weekend in April from the Friday till Monday. Davie set about making plans for his last hurrah as he saw it.

Davie would need to be smart about this one, Billy Angelis had eased up on him it was true but his reach was long and it was deep. One hint of any impropriety and he would be all over him. He couldn't risk going out and being tempted by some wee tidy bit of stuff. No, he would stay in. Get some of the boys off the shift round on the Friday, smoke some blow, drink some Jack Daniels, play some tunes and maybe a few hands of cards, poker or phat. Then on the Saturday he would have a big night. Call some old numbers he still had, get the old faces round and get them to bring some gear and some hookers, a proper big night. That would leave him all day Sunday to recover and get the house back in order for Lucy's return on the Monday.

The Friday night passed off relatively uneventfully. Sure, wee Rab McLuckie had spewed on the fireplace and had to be sent home in a taxi before 10 o'clock and a new fag burn had appeared on the living room carpet but there was nothing that Davie hadn't expected. The young team Jack and Ricky had left the party fairly early to meet their girlfriends up the dancing just after 11. Davie ended up in the conservatory out the back playing a few hands of poker with Gus, Jake and Johnny Toolan, the Eagles playing on the stereo and a couple of well-made joints being passed around. Davie was winning too. Life was good and the main event was still to come tomorrow night and best of all it was all happening well away from the suspicious, prying eyes of one Billy Angelis.

The old faces didn't let Davie down. They arrived with enough gear to blow a hole in Keith Richards' septum, some weed for the comedown and even some ecstasy which had been doing the rounds of the clubs and raves for a while now. Davie made a mental note to try some 'e' as the lads called it at some point. Then there were the hookers, half a dozen of them and all decent lookers although apparently there was a tranny among them, a chick with a dick! At first glance Davie couldn't tell which one it was but he remembered laughing later as wee Gus disappeared into the conservatory with her....or was it him? The party was soon in full swing, JD's and coke all round, lines of Charlie cut up on the glass table and Vanilla Ice and Snap! booming over the music system.

One of a few things Lucy Angelis had in common with her notorious father was that she was headstrong to the point that if she was losing an argument she would storm away rather than admit defeat. On the Saturday of her visit to Dawn the pair had become embroiled in an argument over something trivial that had happened between them at the wedding. In keeping with her nature and even though she had half an inkling she was in the wrong Lucy stormed away to repack her overnight bag. She couldn't believe Dawn was being so unreasonable, after all she had come all this way to see her. Despite Dawn's protests Lucy stormed out of the flat and made for Euston station. As luck would have it a train was leaving for Glasgow within the hour calling at Motherwell en route. Davie would calm her down and soothe her troubles away. She couldn't wait to see him, after all, apart from his nightshift weeks they'd barely spent any time apart. She simply couldn't wait to wrap her arms around him again.

Lucy knew something was up the minute her taxi pulled into the driveway. She'd thought of phoning ahead to let him know of her early return but wanted to surprise him. Every light in the fuckin house was on and music blaring. He was having a party? Occh, so what, it was his house wasn't it, why couldn't he have a few friends round? All the same a sense of dread engulfed Lucy as she placed her hand on the front door and every step she took through the house of horrors her beautiful home had become only added to it. There were strangers everywhere in various states of drunken and utterly raucous states. Nothing though, could quite prepare her for the scene that lay in store for her as she opened her bedroom door. Like a scene from an Amsterdam porn flick, there was some stranger fucking someone doggy style at the bottom of her bed and there lying adjacent was Davie, snorting lines of coke from some whore's tits and there was another one writhing around underneath him. But what was she doing? Licking his arse? Jesus wept! Lucy swallowed back the urge to vomit on the spot and fled silently screaming from the ugly scene before her.

Davie had been aware of someone coming into the room and glanced over. Even in his drug addled, utterly wasted state there was no mistaking the look of hurt, of horror and utter disgust on his wife Lucy's face. It was a look that would haunt him for the rest of his life. What had he done to his beautiful baby and moreover what would Billy Angelis do to him when he found out? He knew there was no point in chasing Lucy down the stairs, knew that his life had just changed forever and not for the better. He hoovered up another line before resolving to clear the debauched scene from his home. Party's fuckin over lads!

When the monumental fuck up that Billy Angelis had half expected from Davie Kellacher duly arrived, two things took him by surprise. The speed of it for one thing, just over 9 months since walking his beautiful daughter down the aisle to that gypsy cunt and he pulls this! Another thing that Billy wasn't quite prepared for was the deep sense of love and anguish he felt for the pain on his poor girl's face. He used that to channel his rage. It had taken all his wife Margaret Ann's skill and cajoling to prevent Billy from going round there and murdering that bastard with his bare hands there and then. 'No, let him live, but make him suffer' she said. 'Think of the effect it would have on poor Lucy. You've worked so hard, why put everything at risk for scum like him?' Of course she was right, his sweet Margaret Ann, fuckin saving him from himself as usual. That gypsy cunt Kellacher would live but Billy would see to it that it was as miserable a fucking existence as possible!

Davie was expecting a kicking, he just didn't know what the extent of it would be and whether or not that would be the end of it, but he suspected not. In truth the boys that Billy sent round the next day were just a little too enthusiastic about their work. 'Just do enough put him in hospital for a few days', had been the instruction. In reality Davie spent 6 weeks in hospital with a ruptured spleen, internal bleeding and some broken ribs. Davie welcomed the pain, it appealed to his natural sense of justice. He had deserved every blow for what he had done to his beautiful Lucy. He'd finally found someone to love and he'd thrown it all away in a coke fuelled binge of self-indulgence. Word came to him that Lucy never wanted to see him again and that cut deeper than any scars Billy's henchmen had left, she didn't even want to have it out with him or ask why. He was to sign everything over to her and Billy would try and get the marriage annulled. Only complete removal of the swarthy, gypsy cunt from the Angelis history books would suffice. Davie hoped against hope that would signal the end of it.

The answer began to become clear to Davie over the following weeks and months. It was obvious to Davie that Billy Angelis was still taking a keen interest in him and over the period his paranoia grew and he found himself constantly on the lookout for trouble. Sure he'd kept a low profile after leaving hospital, going to different pubs, getting out of the shire when he could and heading for the wider expanses of the town. Davie knew deep down there would be more retribution though and his instincts weren't wrong. More than once he'd been on the end of punches seemingly randomly thrown. There was the night in the Heathery Bar, he'd been getting on famously with this gothic looking chick. She was all leather and lace and Davie's libido was stirred for the first time in a while and he couldn't wait to get her home. Then after he'd come back to the table after visiting the toilet and without warning she threw a whole drink over him, slapped his face hard and walked out the door. A couple of ne'er do wells could be seen laughing in the corner. God only knows what they had said to her. He'd taken to heading into Glasgow a lot more often to get out of dodge but the bad luck or Billy's revenge, whatever you may call it, followed him there as well. One night he'd won handsomely at the casino. He was just thinking of booking one of the city centre hotels for the night, scanning the floor to see who the lucky lady might be who might share his bed with some gear and some champagne for a night of fun and frolics when he was approached by an older

Irish gypsy fella. Davie was at ease in this type of company, he'd been around these folk his whole life and loved their tales of travelling and the gypsy life and as a consequence allowed his guard to drop.

When he woke up in the morning, he was in his own bed but had no recollection of how he'd got there. Where were his winnings? He frantically searched his clothes but found not a coin. All he could remember through the fog in his mind was the old gypsy fella laughing as he told him 'Billy sends his regards'. Was it real or had he imagined it? No, the evidence was mounting that a reckoning of some kind was coming. There was no telling where this would all end, face down in a ditch some night for sure. Davie had to get out, enough was enough. The reach of Billy Angelis was long and it was deep but Davie was pretty sure it didn't extend down to the big smoke..........London. So it was that one Friday night Davie Kellacher followed in his father's footsteps and absconded on the night bus to London, with plans never to return.

The boys on shift no 2 knew a little of Davie Kellacher's troubles and there had been plenty of rumours although Jake and Gus who had both been there that fateful night never uttered a word. Most of them had guessed his womanising ways had seen him fall foul of the Angelis clan. None of them delved too deeply though, that wasn't the sort of business you wanted to go wading into. All they knew for sure was that after the kicking he took he was never quite the same guy, quieter, far more withdrawn. You'd see the odd spark of the old Davie sometimes when the guitar came out or there was some pretty girl in the paper but they were fewer and further between. Then one night he called in sick for a Friday nightshift and just a few months before the 'Craig finally closed its gates for good, he was gone. Jack often wondered if he was in a pub in Liverpool or Dublin somewhere. Strumming his guitar singing 'American Pie' or 'The Streets of London' smoking a dooby. Or maybe his broken body was lying at the bottom of a loch somewhere? When you had trodden on the toes of the likes of Billy Angelis all things were possible.....

GOODBYE TO THE SINGLE LIFE

The single life was almost over for Jack Leonard and Ricky Black or rather in the case of Ricky in particular, it already had been for some time, he just wasn't quite aware of it yet. Ricky had been dating Pamela Martin on and off for around two years. Most of the lads were aware of Pamela and had come across her from time to time, they just weren't quite sure of the status of the relationship from one week to the next. Ricky, for his part steadfastly refused to confirm whether or not they were dating or just friends but he would occasionally big her up, calling her his 'soulmate'. Of course Pamela would from time to time become extremely exasperated with this unsatisfactory state of affairs and rebel appropriately, often calling time on their relationship and telling Ricky to find some other 'go to girl.' The problem was Ricky didn't want any other girl and inevitably the pair would pine for one another and after a period of sulking that either or both deemed appropriate they would find their way back together again. Ricky would apologise and promise to be better and Pamela for her part would promise not to give up on him. If you were in a relationship the general rule was Friday nights for chasing and lads nights out and Saturday night was couples night. Simple rules to live your life by. The problem for Ricky was that so many events, both social and sporting would spill over into the time he should have been spending with Pamela. He found it hard to say no to his friends when a big day out at the races was planned or a wee foray into Glasgow. It was a constant source of arguments between the pair how much time he spent at football, golf, horse racing and a myriad of other pastimes woven into the fabric of Ricky's social life whilst Pamela wondered if she was just an incidental extra in it all.

Gradually though, Ricky began to learn how to say no to his friends on occasion and he began to extricate himself from the late nights that would inevitably end in some kebab shop at 3am or an early morning drinking session in someone's flat. He would just disappear in a club and later it would emerge that he had gone to Pamela's. Pretty soon he was leaving before he got anywhere near the nightclub doors and before too long he was dipping out altogether on the sacred lads night out on a Friday as well. Yes, Ricky Black had fallen for Pamela Martin, maybe not fallen hard the way some lads do but he had fallen under her spell just the same and had become heavily reliant on her and her warmth and kindness and that way she nuzzled into his neck making him feel like a million dollars! For her part, she worried about him, worried about his gambling and his reputation as the unluckiest gambler on shift no 2 .She worried about the way he clung to his notoriety amongst the lads as such, but most of all she worried about him working in 'that' place. She had seen the state of him one night he'd come home to her after accompanying one of the lads up to hospital in an ambulance after an accident at the furnace, couldn't believe the colour of him. He'd laughed it all off as usual, doing an Al Jolson jazz hands impression as though he was a fuckin minstrel, but she could see deeper into him and how it was affecting him. They were all dreading it, the day the axe fell and the 'Craig closing its gates forever, but she wasn't. She'd be glad to have her precious Ricky out of there safe and sound and they'd get by just fine.

The single life for a young man on the shifts offered a multitude of options and not all of them involved drinking, smoking and gambling either, although inevitably sometimes these vices found their way in. Snooker was one such pastime and on the shift the game was popular and there would be occasional snooker days out at the Fir Park Club or the Horse and Anchor. Regularly, usually off the dayshift, the lads Jack and Ricky would go to the snooker hall in Hamilton, the Big Break. They would always play the first to five frames and Ricky being Ricky decided it would be better to introduce 'a wee interest' and they would play for a fiver a frame. Of course on a bad day that meant you could be down to the tune of 25 quid but mercifully that didn't happen too often as both Ricky and Jack were generally equally as hopeless at the game as each other. Another popular pastime for the lads was golf or the 'gowf' as they called it. Some of the marrieds on the shift had golf memberships at some of the many Lanarkshire clubs. Tommy Wilson and the 'Chief' were members at Wishaw and Marky Dunlop at Bellshill. The boys would go for a round generally off the nightshift, early in the morning when the courses were quiet and the sun had just come up. They were both fair weather golfers and of course Scotland being prone to the odd bout of precipitation, often rain stopped their plans in their tracks but when the weather played fair all the men found the fresh air and calm of the golf course a perfect antidote to the dust and clatter of the furnace.

If they were evenly matched on the snooker table, you could safely say that Ricky and Jack were poles apart on a golf course. Ricky was by any standard a good steady golfer and regularly played to a handicap of 15 and sometimes a good deal better. Jack though was a hacker. Capable of occasional brilliance he generally hit the ball well enough but there were usually too many 7's or 8's on his card or sometimes worse. It was a constant source of frustration to Jack how he could play some really good shots one minute and then be utterly hopeless the next, every amateur golfers curse! Even on the rare occasion when Jack had put it all together to shoot a more than respectable 87 at Wishaw, Ricky had typically gone one better shooting an 86! It was on the golf course that Ricky had first seen unusual glimpses of Jack's temper being lost. On one occasion playing at Bellshill with Marky Dunlop, Jack had struck two excellent shots on the 18th hole to reach the green in the regulation 2. He only needed 2 putts for a rare par, no mean feat on a difficult hole. The greens were fast that day after an unusually long dry spell and Jack had difficulty reading them. This way and that Jack rolled his ball hopelessly past much to Dunlop's amusement and after missing at his fourth attempt Jack snapped and threw his club down. It bounced off at an angle and the heel of the putter took a huge divot out of the green. One of the members watching from the clubhouse must have grassed them up and the blazers, the committee men, were waiting for them when they came off and told them none too politely they wouldn't be welcomed back. Marky Dunlop was furious with Jack as well, as the blazers threatened to revoke his membership, but fuck him and the blazer clad gestapo as well. In truth neither Jack nor Ricky had any time for Dunlop. He was a bullshitter, a storyteller. It didn't matter where you'd been or what you'd done, he had always been somewhere better or done something even more remarkable. Na, fuck him and his poxy golf club. At least if they were barred from Bellshill they wouldn't need to listen to him spouting his pish for 18 holes any more the boys laughed later.

Ricky and Jack preferred playing at Wishaw with Tommy Wilson and the 'Chief'. The chat was easier and more relaxed as they made their way round the course in considerably more amiable company. Tommy was a great guy, everyone liked him. He was knowledgeable about all the subjects the boys were interested in and even though he was married with kids he still liked a night out and had brilliant banter. The Chief by comparison was much more serious and seemed much more grown up to the lads but he was always interesting to talk to and had such a breadth of knowledge about a variety of subjects that they always felt as though they were learning from him. Not in a teacher/pupil kind of way though, the Chief was a mate and always gave the impression that he would always do the boys a good turn if he could. Any time that the quartet went for a game off the dayshift Chief or Tommy would offer to drive and the lads were able to pack a few beers into their bag as an added bonus. One thing about walking around Wishaw golf course though, was that it afforded a panoramic view of the 'Craig from almost every vantage point. An almost constant reminder of the shifts that lay ahead or whatever nightmare they'd just endured. It was not surprising at all then that the lads would occasionally venture further afield into the countryside. Polkemmet, Shotts and Fauldhouse golf courses were all a short drive away and as luck would have it Ricky knew the golf pro at Fauldhouse.

One morning Ricky and Jack were running a little late for a Saturday morning round at Fauldhouse. The pro that Ricky knew at the course would let them on at the weekend just before the club medal (a weekly competition for members) went out but

Ricky's neebur that morning had been Gerry Bonner and he'd been a good half hour late after sinking a few too many in the Railway Tavern in Motherwell the night before. Some of the members had already assembled at the first tee by the time Ricky and Jack arrived and were huddled around marking their details on their scorecards and chattering about the sort of mundane shite serious golfers talk about. 'You two are late but if ye get a shifty on there's just about enough time', said Ricky's mate. The boys hurried to the first tee and by now the small assembly of early morning golfers had grown to quite a throng. Jack glanced nervously around at the small gathering. He hated a crowd watching him at the first tee and he hated being hurried. 'I'll go first', he said quickly to Ricky, in a hurry to get this over with and get off down the fairway far away from critical eyes. Jack had a quick practice swing then swung wildly at the ball completely fresh airing it. Mortified, Jack addressed the ball again hoping no one had noticed and there was a deathly hush behind him but he felt sure he could make out a few muffled titters. The drizzle had started to fall as they had arrived and the grip on Jack's driver was wet now but there was no time to fuck about with towels at the moment. Jack let fly again this time connecting with the ball but he had 'topped' it forcing the ball down into the ground before it bounced on the tee and dribbled just a few yards down the fairway. Worse than that though, on the follow through Jack felt his grip loosen and the club flew out of his hand somersaulting through the air before coming to rest high up in the branches of the big tree some ten yards to his left. This time there was no mistaking the guffaws and howls of laughter from the golfers behind as one of them shouted 'I've a ladder in my van if ye want tae go up and get that'. Even Ricky could barely control himself as it came his turn to tee off, his shoulders shaking up and down as he tried to regain his composure. Typically then as things settled down momentarily he fired a near perfect drive straight down the middle. As the boys threw their bags over their shoulders to head off one of the golfers shouted 'You no going up the tree now for your club?' 'It can fuckin stay there', Jack snapped back as he stomped off. He barely stopped to take his second shot scuffing another poor effort 50 yards or so further on. He just wanted out of here away from these fuckers. Jack was having a nightmare and the boys had to let three groups of players go past them on the course as they were holding everyone up. They were spared further embarrassment by the latest group behind arguing over a lost ball and Jack was at last able to relax a bit and even laugh at some of his earlier misfortune with Ricky. He duly continued to hack his way round the rest of the course until finally he caught a peach of a drive on the 18th tee. Maybe he was going to finish with a flourish at least? Alas with his second shot he shanked the ball wildly to his left towards the car park and the boys looked at one another in horror as they heard a loud thwack! 'Fuck, that sounded like a windscreen' said Ricky. 'Let's get the fuck out of here!' With that they grabbed their bags and were offski, even by Jack's standards it had been a poor day on the course. One thing was for sure, when it came to the golf Ricky definitely had the upper hand over his friend.

There were other pastimes that the lads on the shift indulged in as well. Tommy Wilson would often book the 5 a sides halls at Eddlewood Sports Barn or Larkhall if they could muster enough players for a game, occasionally co-opting some of the boys from the other rotas if the shifts allowed. A new gym had opened up above Faces nightclub and Jack and Ricky would frequent it from time to time trying not to look too out of place amongst the boxers and martial arts exponents who were regulars. There were also sporadic visits to the swimming baths at Larkhall and Hamilton as the lads occasionally debated their fitness levels and their excessive alcohol consumption. Talk of a day or night out was never far away though and either side of the Clyde in Lanarkshire or a short train hop into Glasgow there were a world of different choices. Whenever your day off fell on the continental shift pattern the lads followed, there was always somewhere that you could go to blow off some steam or in the case of two young single men......go on the chase!

There were two distinct categories in the late night world of the young free and single of the 'shire. There were the dedicated nightclubs with their neon signs and soft lighting and mirrored walls and dry ice. Places to get dressed up for and to be seen in. Then, there were the working men's clubs and the social clubs where the prices were cheaper, the clientele were generally but not always older and the atmosphere leaning towards the more laid back variety and somewhat less intense.

A jaunt into Glasgow was always something of an event for the boys and they would don their best clobber and sink a few beers on the train on the way in. There always seemed to be a different atmosphere in town, more vibrant and more cosmopolitan and of course the range of choice was on a completely different scale from back home in Lanarkshire. The lads had their firm favourites though having sampled many of the options available. One of those, on the banks Clydeside was the Pier 39 although Jack had fallen out of love with it one night when the DJ had started singing 'No, No. No, No, No, No….there's no trophies to the tune of 2Unlimited's 'No Limit'. It was a clear dig at his beloved Celtic's poor season and Jack considered it unprofessional and even went looking for the manager to complain. Ricky couldn't understand the what big deal was and eventually got Jack to calm down and laugh it off, after all the Clydeside was designated 'Rangers' territory and the Tims had their own places in the Merchant City and up the Gallowgate. Further uptown in the city centre the Brahms and Liszt was another favourite. A basement pub, it covered all the bases with the bar area being a great spot for pulling as groups of guys and girls often met up there as a starting point for the night. The boys would often attempt to hone their chat up technique in this very spot, also perfecting the art of looking windswept and interesting whilst leaning at the bar. The Brahms also doubled as a good spot to take a date. The 'L' shaped bar with checker board flooring that played tricks with your eyes as the alcohol took hold, opened out into a dimly lit lounge area with old round mahogany tables scattered around hosting lit church candles dripping in wax. It was a perfect spot for a romantic interlude spoiled only by the occasional whiff of the Renfield Street drains.

Further up uptown and near the top of the hill along the infamous Sauchiehall Street or sausage roll street as the boys called it, lay Victoria's and the 'Suave Sav' or Savoy. 'If you cannae get yer hole in there , ye may as well cut it aff', Jack remembered the legendary lothario Davie Kellacher advising him. Sure enough the Savoy was a prime pulling venue and you were just as likely to get lucky on its infamous office party night on a Wednesday as you were on a Friday and Saturday night. Mind you Davie had also told that the boys that the Savoy was near enough impossible to get chucked out of yet Ricky had somehow managed just that one night. He had been wandering round the dancefloor looking for Jack who had seemingly disappeared. In fact Jack was in the disabled toilet throwing up after one too many and talking to God on the big white telephone. On his third circuit of the floor looking for Jack, Ricky had drawn the attention of the bouncers and as he fiddled in his pocket for chewing gum he was grabbed and taken to the office as the staff suspected him of dealing drugs. After searching him they were just about to apologise when one of them, eyeing him warily said 'how much you had to drink fella?' In typically quick witted fashion Ricky replied 'whit's this noo, a fuckin quiz?' At that they bundled him out of the office and manhandled him into the lift and down the stairs into the cold night air with one or two digs to the ribs as a parting gift! If the 'Suave Sav' (sarcastically named) was the venue of choice for the working classes, then Victoria's, at least in its heyday, was the place to be for the well-heeled, the footballers and the wannabe wags. A poseurs paradise Tommy Wilson had called it. Sure enough Jack had seen his fair share of famous faces in the place. A place where the Glasgow glitterati and its gangsters mixed freely. One Friday night Jack had even seen the Celtic star Paul Elliot pouring his inebriated teammate Darius Dziekanowski into a taxi and the night before a game as well! Sure enough when the team lines were read out at Parkhead the next day Dziekanowski was missing with a mysterious injury!

Back in the shire and in the social clubs there were different strokes for different folks….Friday nights for chasing and Saturday night was couples night, an unwritten law that was universally understood. The social clubs generally relied on live bands for entertainment and for a good band the Lanarkshire gigging circuit could be a lucrative one. Of course Fridays and Saturdays were the big nights as with everywhere else, with Airdrie Workmen's, Fir Park and the Cleland club particular favourites of the lads. Sunday afternoons were for the hangover curer with the Burnbank Masonic and Greenfield Club popular venues. Monday nights at the Cleland club were legendary nights out if you had the day off and a late start on the Tuesday. Wednesday was grab a Granny night at the Bellshill Miners if you couldn't be bothered with the trek into town to the 'Suave.' In truth there weren't many 'grannies' there, rather the place was full of middle aged divorcees looking for fun and there were rich pickings for a young single man with disposable income. There was a totally different vibe in the social clubs, a sort of underground culture where the older generation, the divorcees and the married and cheating came together to let their hair down and get away from whatever fuckin hum drum existences they were leading and the lads soon discovered there was much fun to be had in joining the fray. Of course another big advantage that the working men's clubs held was cost. You could get a pint and a chaser for less than some of the nightclubs would charge for a bottle of beer. Some of the clubs though still went in for peculiarities that irked the boys at times. Traditions that had been handed down from generation to generation. There were the committee men with their club blazers on who thought they were fuckin God, telling you to get your feet off the seat or that you were queueing at the wrong side of the bar, little fuckin Hitlers full of their own self-importance. Other traditions as well, such as half time bingo or standing for a national anthem at the end of the night had no place on the social scene as far as Ricky and Jack were concerned, not when you were trying to get your hole for fucks sake!

If the working men's clubs had a certain charm, it's fair to say that they couldn't compete with the talent on offer in the dedicated nightclubs across the shire. A younger crowd dressed to impress, an edgier atmosphere and the dimly lit corners full of sexual intent were like a magnet for the lads of a weekend. They were semi regulars at Faces in Motherwell. It was a short hop from the 'Craig if you were off a backshift and the lads were on first name terms with the doormen so there was never any question over possibly not gaining entry. Also they liked the DJ, he seemed to have the pulse of the place and knew just when to put on the floorfillers and the fuck me tunes full of sexual innuendo. Crucially, the lads strike rate in terms of pulling in Faces was better than average. They had fall back options in Faces as well. There was Debbie Poderis, a statuesque blond from a family with a fearsome reputation in North Motherwell. Debbie had her own flat though and would often host after parties and she wasn't too fussy who she ended up spending the night with and the boys joked that they were now officially half-brothers after both having spent the night with her. Then there was Vera Lee or the 'Kinky Chinky' as the boys had nicknamed her. Vera was very much a free spirit with a libido that was more than a match for any man and she had fucked her way through most of the decent looking blokes amongst the Faces clientele. She wasn't even Chinese as it happened with her family hailing from Thailand, but misogyny and casual racism were alive and well in 1990's Lanarkshire even if no one cared to admit it. Ah well, ignorance is bliss as they say, or in this case, just ignorance. Yes, Faces was a firm favourite with the lads!

Another handy go to venue for late night adventures was the Commercial in Wishaw, albeit for different reasons. The Commercial had something of a reputation for letting anyone in any state in, a sort of get out jail free card when all other possibilities had been exhausted. It also had the reputation of being a great pulling venue especially if ladies of somewhat looser morals were your thing. So, if you had been out on the lash all day and were on your last legs it was an option rather than risk the dreaded 'not tonight lads' at the door elsewhere.

One night when the lads were off the backshift Jack had witnessed Ricky successfully pulling a tidy blond who went by the name of Eve. Still dressed in his donkey style RFD jacket, his lashes still thick with the dust and stoor from a shift on the highline, he'd taken her back to her flat in Muirhouse afterwards but he got more pussy than he had bargained for. The lady in question was a cat lover but Ricky was allergic. He felt the tell-tale signs almost immediately, his eyes puffing up and an urgent need to sneeze but resolved to power on through, after all 'yar holes yar hole.' As he struggled with the buttons on the front of her dress as they lay on the couch together, he began to blink uncontrollably, attempting to suppress the inevitable, but there was no stopping it. Finally, he let it go....an enormous sneeze all over her face. As he surveyed the sticky mess that resembled a cum shot from a German porno shoot Ricky grimaced and was forced to admit defeat. 'Sorry doll, I don't think this is gonnae work out', he made his excuses and headed for home. On another occasion Jack had landed in the Commercial with Gerry Bonner after a near all day session encompassing most of the boozers on Wishaw Main Street. It had been a baking hot day made all the hotter by the molten metal Jack had been working with all morning. He knew he wasn't looking his best or smelling his sweetest but as always in the Commercial there was always some lady willing to respond to Jack's roving eye and winning smile. The lucky lady in question this night was a 38 year old divorcee, Lorraine from Coltness, looking for fun and a quick boost to her ego and Jack was more than happy to oblige. The pair were soon frantically tugging at one anothers clothing in the back of the taxi. When they arrived at the house Jack quickly removed his shoes noticing the thick cream shag pile carpet in the living room. Lorraine immediately screwed up her face. 'Jesus', she said. 'I'm telling you now, nothing's gonnae happen till ye wash they feet, they're absolutely fuckin honking!' 'Eh?' replied Jack incredulously. Nonetheless he allowed Lorraine to lead him into the bathroom and just as Jesus had done for his disciples, she washed his feet. The drama wasn't finished there though. Lorraine had led on into the bedroom and taken control, straddling a now more sweetly smelling Jack and began to ride him slowly and tantalisingly. Suddenly, Jack heard the unmistakable sound of the front door opening and someone bounding up the stairs. 'Oh, you've got company', said a figure in the doorway. 'Who the fuck is that?' said Jack in a mild state of terror. 'That's my hubby' said Lorraine matter of factly and slowly began moving rhythmically on top of him again. 'I thought you were divorced?' enquired a now seriously concerned Jack his voice rising several octaves. 'Oh we are, we're just waiting to sell the house,' said Lorraine becoming breathless with excitement at the show she was putting on. 'Mind if I watch?' said the figure in the doorway. 'Fine by me,' replied Lorraine barely able to answer and now riding Jack frantically on the verge of orgasm. Soon the figure in the doorway had edged closer and appeared astride Lorraine pushing his cock into her mouth. Fuck me! This is a new experience and no mistake thought Jack, but he embraced the surreal experience and for hours to come, he and the figure in the doorway, who turned out be called Ian, fucked the insatiable Lorraine in every way imaginable.

How the boys of shift number 2 laughed as Ricky and Jack exchanged their tales of debauchery and disaster in the bothy back at the furnace. For some there was a tinge of envy at their escapades but for the biggest majority it made them grateful for the loving wives and family life they had at home away from all that fuckin madness! Away from the easy pickings of the Commercial and Faces there were plenty of other choices open to the boys when they felt the need of a change of scenery. There was the Zanzi Bar in Airdrie, a big barn of a place and by contrast a few hundred yards along the road Diamonds which had the feel of an underground bunker, a party in someones basement. There was the Club De France in Coatbridge which boasted sets from Radio Clyde DJ's and pulled big crowds as a result. Across the water in Hamilton, the Rococco Club and Park Lane were amongst the first places to offer the boys a taste of club nightlife and were old favourites as a result. All over the shire and into the town the boys had tasted almost all that there was to offer and what times they'd had and what stories they could tell, but all that was coming to an end now, the single life was over.

If Ricky Black had gradually drifted away from the single life, then you could say that Jack Leonard positively hopped, skipped and bounded away from it after a chance encounter at the Rococco Club in Hamilton one Friday night. It had been one of those nights that seemed to be heading nowhere, in fact Jack had been considering making the best of a bad job and calling it a night. After a bright start on the horses Ricky had predictably lost heavily as usual, then just as predictably his mood had brightened (whit's fur ye'll no go by ye) and he had become the life and soul of the party such as it was. There was a lively crowd in the Lud that night and it had been further bolstered by a few lads from no 3 shift in off the backshift. In no time at all it seemed the clock had beaten them all and it was time to stick or twist…….home time or time to head for the dancing. 'Let's go to Hamilton, we huvnae been over there for ages' reasoned Ricky. 'I have heard good things about the Rococco on a Friday night', Jack agreed a little reluctantly and so it was set, a taxi to Hamilton and a night on the tiles it was. The Rococco was a relatively new venture in the town but Jack had liked it the few times he'd been in. You had to go up a flight of stairs to get in but once you were in it was a place that had a more intimate feel to it than many of the other Lanarkshire clubs like Faces or Club de France or Zanzi Bar. It was smaller and narrower than most but the raised level at the end where the cocktail bar was gave it an air of Glasgow city centre sophistication. The dance floor was to your left as you walked in banked by a mirrored wall and the bar was to your right. Jack took in the scene with a smile as the music (not too loud) set the beat on the dancefloor and the first few puffs of dry ice tickled the back of his throat. Ricky ghosted past him making the enquiry as to what he wanted to drink using only his hands and Jack responded making the big glass sign indicating he wanted a pint rather than a short. Then he turned his gaze towards the dancefloor and it was then that he saw her. It was hard to tell exactly what colour hair she had with all the neon and u.v. light glowing against the mirrored wall. What he could see was that it was long, curly tumbling down on her shoulders in spiral waves. What he could also see, was the way she was moving to the music, it was hypnotic and he'd never seen anything quite like it and it was clear to him that she was lost in the music, not caring who was watching yet almost every movement was overtly sexual or so it seemed to Jack. Black Box, 'Ride on fuckin Time' indeed thought Jack as he shifted his position to get a better look. She was wearing a tight, short black dress matched with knee high boots which just added to Jack's excitement and he resolved to make a move as soon as Ricky came back with the drinks. Normally, Jack was a ditherer, waiting for the right moment, debating his chat up line or best approach, sometimes even waiting till the end of the night when he'd taken enough Dutch courage. Not tonight. Tonight, he would be decisive and proactive from the beginning. It's as well he was too, for he wasn't the only admirer in the club to make a play that night for this hot mess.

Rachel Dines was to be no pushover for Jack either. She had met some of these steelworker boys before with their fat wallets and their trendy clothes. The 'Craig was on borrowed time though and soon these big time Charlies would be unemployment statistics and Rachel knew it. There was something different about this boy though with his kind smile and piercing blue eyes. He'd have to work for it though, she wasn't quite playing hard to get but he wouldn't be getting the full on snog he'd been angling for since easing in beside her on the dancefloor twenty minutes ago and breathlessly charming her with sweet compliments whispered in her ear.

They did kiss eventually, as the patrons began to head for the cloakrooms and the bar staff began to tidy away the empties. Then just as Jack thought she might leave him high and dry she leaned in and pulled him to her. She had teased him right up until the last moment about seeing him again at the taxi rank as well, finally slipping her number into his hand just as the taxi was about to pull away. 'Call me tomorrow', she said. He did and so it began, Jack was officially off the market.

Pretty soon Jack found himself courting the advice of the married men on the shift, asking them about where was good to take someone for dinner or what films were good at the cinema at the moment and even if there were any good plays worth seeing at the theatre. His whole social outlook had suddenly changed and all in a bid to impress the lovely lady in his life, and she was definitely impressed. Why wouldn't she be? Tickets were bought for plays and comedy shows at the Pavilion in Glasgow, dinner reservations at Da Luciano in Bothwell or La Fiorentina in Glasgow and weekends away in romantic Paris and cosmopolitan London were arranged. Yes, Jack Leonard was pulling out all the stops and it was having the desired effect as the pair fell headlong into the realms of becoming a serious couple. There was just one fly in the ointment. From very early on in their relationship Jack had known he wanted to marry this girl. However Rachel's family were a family at war and a big wedding would likely become no more than a battleground, an opportunity to settle old scores. To that end Rachel had made it quite clear that she had no desire to be the centrepiece of any such occasion. It was a thorny problem and Jack often had to bite back his urgent need and desire to pop the question as a result. However in the months ahead outside events would take a hand and present Jack with the perfect solution to his dilemma.

WHEN HEROES BECAME LEGENDS AND RICKY BLACK LOST HIS SHIRT

The events of the 18th May 1991 on the pitch at Hampden Park and thereafter on the streets and in the pubs and clubs of Motherwell are the stuff of legend. A town haunted by the spectre of the closure of its lifeblood got to throw off the shackles of impending doom and party in the sun, even if it was for just one weekend. Inter connected to these events and playing in parallel to them, the boys of shift no 2 were involved in their own little dramatic sideshow that day, played out in the bothy of no 1 furnace.

To fully understand how events unfolded the way they did it's necessary to go back a few months before to Scottish Cup 3rd round day and an away tie for Motherwell at cup holders Aberdeen. The lads were dayshift that day and from the moment they began arriving for their shift wee Johnny Toolan was proclaiming 'Motherwell's gonnae win the cup, am tellin yeez, get yer money oan it, this is the year, Motherwell's gonnae win the cup!' It goes without saying Johnny was a Motherwell fan, although not the type whose devotion extended to attending actual football matches these days. He had at one time but stopped attending after breaking his ankle in a crush at Fir Park when Fulham came visiting for an Anglo Scottish Cup tie laden with football aristocrats like Georgie Best and Rodney Marsh. It was a story he rarely tired of telling, of his brush with near death at Fir Park, but these days the extent of his devotion to the claret and amber was telling everyone on no 2 shift 'Motherwell's gonnae win the day' or as in the case today, on Scottish Cup 3rd Round day, 'Motherwell's gonnae win the cup' and so it would continue until Motherwell were inevitably knocked out. Considering the opening assignment Motherwell had been handed today even fewer than normal paid any attention to wee Johnny's mutterings, but Motherwell did win. Stevie Kirk stepped off the bench and with his first touch smashed a winning goal that ended holders Aberdeen's defence of the cup and set Motherwell on the road to Hampden.

Johnny Toolan was very much a man of dual identities. To the boys on shift no 2 he was the shift pervert, an amenable if frighteningly intense character at times, the go to guy for an array of eye watering porn that covered all tastes and all genres. As much as he cultivated this image and would embellish it where possible, the truth was that Johnny rarely if ever watched any of this junk and in fact wouldn't even have it in the house for fear any of his kids came across it. He did though, supplement his income by trading in videos, CD roms , floppy disks etc from a contact he had at Wishaw market and it was a lucrative outlet too, for some of the lads had an insatiable appetite for porn and other pirated movies. No, despite what the lads may have thought Johnny Toolan was very much a family man, devoted to his wife Eleanor and their three kids Abbey, Lisa and the apple of his eye, wee Sammy.

Johnny did though however delight in cultivating his image as an 'Arthur Daley' type character with serious perversions to boot. It amused him to see the young lads squirm as he told them of some new masturbation techniques he'd been trying out. On one occasion he had the young lads Jack and Ricky trapped in the corner of the bothy as he excitedly told them the tale of his morning wank. 'Honest lads, yeez need tae try this. There ah wis, wan leg up on the toilet seat or ye could use the side ae the bath, the other leg planted. Once ye get tae the tickly bit yer standing leg buckles underneath ye and ye fall backwards and hit yer heid on the floor whilst jizzin all over yerself. Its fuckin magic, exhaustin but. Ye shid try it oot the night', laughed Johnny as Ricky and Jack recoiled in horror and tried in vain to remove the potent images now flashing through their minds. He was also the first person anyone had ever heard mention asphyxiation and choking themselves to orgasm as a technique. 'Yeez need tae try this, tie a scarf roon the headboard then roon yer neck. As ye pull yirself aff, move doon the bed so the knot gits tighter and tighter, by the time yer ready tae cum ye feel as though yer gonnae pop yer eyeballs oot. Amazin!' In truth Johnny had heard all this stuff from the nutters he associated with down the market but the lads of shift no 2 weren't to know that and anyway he just loved the shock value and the looks of absolute horror on some of the lads faces when he got fully into character.

Meanwhile Motherwell's progression through the rounds of the cup continued and might have gone largely unnoticed if it weren't for the increasingly noisy proclamations from one Johnny Toolan that 'this was their year'. The exit of one of the 'big two' from the cup always provided that extra bit of stimulus for the other clubs, in theory leaving a clearer route to the final for someone at least. So, when Celtic and Rangers were paired to face one another in the quarter finals at Celtic Park, Johnny Toolan's ramblings became louder still and began to irritate one of the lads on the shift in particular…….. a certain Ricky Black.

Something else that irritated Ricky was that Celtic had defeated his beloved Rangers 2-0 to march through to the semi-finals and were now in pole position to claim the Cup. Motherwell though had also made it through, albeit in less convincing style beating first division sides Falkirk and Morton, the latter with the aid of a replay and a penalty shootout and now Celtic awaited them in the semi-final. Ricky Black finally lost patience with Johnny Toolan's bravado over a game of cards in no1 bothy one Friday nightshift.

As he dealt the cards Johnny quipped 'Motherwell's nearly there, the cups in the bag lads'. Ricky took the bait. 'Aye in your dreams ya wee perv' he replied. Johnny smiled, delighted young Ricky had fallen into his trap, 'It'll no be the Rangers anyway this year, cos they're fuckin oot!', he laughed as did the others present in the bothy. Ricky bristled at the dig, he'd had enough of this. 'If you're so sure it's gonnae be Motherwell's year why don't ye put your money where yer mouth is' he challenged. 'Oh, a wee wager is it son?' Johnny asked lifting his gaze momentarily from his hand and genuinely surprised that young Ricky was so rattled. 'What ye got in mind son, a wee tenner on the outcome of the semi?' asked Toolan as he slid his hand across the table to shake on it. 'A tenner? Na, that's school playground stuff. If you're so convinced let's make it something worthwhile. I'll tell you what, 50 quid says Celtic will win the semi and am even that confident I'll give you the benefit of the draw!' Ricky announced emphatically, confident he had put mouthy Toolan's gas firmly at a peep. Johnny scratched his beard for a moment somewhat taken aback. He didn't mind a wee gamble now and again, but only after Eleanor had been sorted out with the housekeeping and whatever else she needed and the kids with their pocket money and even then, this kind of wager was unusual and a bit too rich for him. The eyes of the rest of the shift were on him now though, his bravado had been called into question and he felt backed into a corner. He looked young Ricky in the eye and made as if to spit in his right hand and then put it forward to seal the deal. 'I'll take that bet son', he said nonchalantly, '50 quid says Motherwell's gonnae win and I get the draw as well'. 'Deal', snapped Ricky as the two shook on it………..the wager was set.

The semi-final took place some 10 days later and as the lads were on a day off Jack was able to attend the game. Predictably Celtic dominated much of the play but created very little in the way of goal scoring chances and as a result Motherwell began to grow in confidence. As the game wore on it became clear that one goal for either side would win it and in a frantic closing period both sides had penalty claims turned down, Celtic had an effort kicked off the line and Ferguson struck the post with an audacious free kick effort for Motherwell. When the referee called time though, the scoresheet remained blank and the teams would have to do it all again in a replay. Jack threw his hands up in exasperation then smiled as he thought of his friend Ricky and the bet with Toolan. The wee man had fucked it again thought Jack, giving Toolan the benefit of the draw had been unnecessarily stupid. He shook his head at the lunacy of it all as he headed for the exits at Hampden.

Most of the lads on shift no 2 had become aware of the bet struck by Johnny Toolan and Ricky Black and those who congregated around no 1 furnace were keen to see the exchange between the pair as the bet was settled and they weren't to be disappointed. Wee Johnny was sitting in the bothy nonchalantly peeling an orange as the shift began to trickle in and more than a few picked their spot to see what would unfold. Johnny was aware of the circus around him and whilst he was quietly enjoying the notoriety, in truth he had no desire to take money from young Ricky and felt bad about it. But, a bet was a bet and you always paid your dues, it was one of those unwritten golden rules. Simple rules to live your life by. The excitable chatter in the bothy became somewhat muted as Ricky strolled in. He made straight for Johnny Toolan and sat across from him a smile spreading across his face. 'Ya jammy wee fucker' Ricky teased. 'Aww come on, it wis a fair result', replied Johnny. Ricky delved into his pocket and eased a small pile of ten pound notes across the table towards Johnny but stopped halfway, covering the money with the palm of his hand. 'You could take that' said Ricky 'or……we could let it ride on the replay, double or quits!' There were muffled chuckles from the assembled onlookers scattered around the bothy but Ricky's reasoning was simple and well founded. Celtic were the big favourites here. Motherwell had missed their chance and they wouldn't likely get another in the replay, after all Celtic never lost replays. Any sane Motherwell fan would take the money and run but Ricky had teased Toolan into the bet in the first place by calling his bravado into question, maybe he could tease him into it again and get himself out of dodge at the same time. Toolan considered the proposal aware that the eyes of the shift were on him again. Frankly, Johnny reckoned that Ricky's reasoning was probably correct and that the 'Well were unlikely to get a second bite at the mighty Glasgow Celtic, but he had no real desire to take money from the young man opposite him anyway. So, if it gave young Ricky an opportunity to hang onto his money and at the same time show the rest of the lads he had the courage of his convictions, there was no real reason to turn the wager down, it was the perfect get out clause for everyone. 'Double or quits it is then young Ricky, just don't come crying tae me when ye need tae hand over a hundred quid' said Johnny as he slid the money back across the table and the pair shook hands to seal the deal. The rest of the onlookers let out a little cheer and with relief Ricky folded the little pile of notes he had proffered back into his pocket.

The replay was set for Hampden Park in a week's time and as the lads were dayshift Jack was again able to attend the match. It was to be one of his most frustrating evenings watching Celtic ever. Oh it started well enough and Celtic poured forward to good effect causing havoc in the Motherwell defence. Elliot scored an early goal, but no, it was disallowed for offside but Motherwell's relief was only temporary and Celtic were soon ahead. Rather than go and kill the game off though Celtic let Motherwell back in it and Arnott equalised. Again Celtic poured forward and the chances kept coming, eventually Rogan made it 2-1 and Coyne missed a golden chance for 3-1 but surely now Celtic had Motherwell on the ropes? At half time most of the Hampden crowd could only see one winner. In the second half though all the zip had seemingly gone from Celtic legs and it was Motherwell who were beginning to dominate. Jack watched on in horror then near disbelief as first Arnott levelled again then Colin O'Neill, a big brick shit house of a boy that Motherwell fans affectionately termed as 'Psycho', let a shot go from all of 30 or 40 yards (depending on who you believe), Bonner threw himself across goal in vain, his flailing arm nowhere near it and the unthinkable was suddenly happening. A few minutes later and the unthinkable was confirmed when Kirk curled in an effort caught by the wind, Bonner left stranded. Jack was resigned to his fate, when you lost goals like that you just had to hold your hands up and concede it just wasn't your day. As the Motherwell end celebrated wildly Jack began to trudge home through the mucky Glasgow night, so gutted that temporarily at least he had completely forgotten about his friend Ricky and the 'bet'.

The boys on shift no 2 hadn't forgotten though and all the excitable chatter at the newsagents in Craigneuk as the boys picked up their morning rolls and Daily Records and at the clocks as the boys stamped their time cards in and out, was of last night's events and what turn the 'wager' might take now. They didn't have to wait long to find out. As before Johnny Toolan was in his usual perch at the seat in the corner next to the wall in no 1 bothy, this time nursing an early morning cup of coffee. Ricky Black walked into a suddenly hushed bothy, 'Well this is a fuckin turn up for the books, should've known better than tae bet on the Celtic!' he said loudly a smile spreading across his face. It was a display of bravado few could have matched given the circumstances. Johnny simply smiled and shook his head aware again that the eyes of the shift were upon them. As before Ricky sat down opposite Johnny and delved into his jacket pocket to produce a small pile of crisp £10 notes fresh from the cashline. As before he slid the money into the middle of the table and then stopped, covering the cash with the palm of his hand. 'I could give you this..............but, if you're so sure this is Motherwell's year, why not let it ride. Double or quits on the final!' Ricky said emphatically holding out his hand to seal the deal. Johnny shook his head, what fresh fuckin madness was this? The rest of the lads let out an excitable roar and in unison began to chatter about the merits of this fresh challenge before hushing down quickly to hear Johnny's response. Ricky's reasoning was again simple enough. Motherwell's opponents in the final would be Dundee United who had beaten St. Johnstone in the other semi- final. United were a better side, they had finished two places above Motherwell in the league and had beaten them in four out their five meetings that season. Of course there was the small matter of fact that under present manager Jim McLean they had lost five successive finals at Hampden but in the style of a true optimist Ricky had brushed that aside, reasoning that 'they were due one!' As before, Johnny Toolan had no desire to take any money off young Ricky and it was true this would give him a way out, but this whole thing was getting way out of hand. Johnny sighed and shifted uncomfortably in his seat aware of the eyes on him. 'Fuck sake wee man, that's 200 quid you're intae now. You sure that's whit ye want?' Johnny put the ball back in Ricky's court half hoping he would call a halt to this charade but his heart racing at the thrill of it all. Ricky pushed his hand forward again and the pair shook on it to loud cheers in the bothy. Fuckin hell, they were going again! Double or quits on the final, the gossip raged around the furnace and beyond!

The build up to the cup final was of one befitting a town like Motherwell. In the absence of either Celtic or Rangers who both carried a big support in the area, it seemed like the whole town was able to get behind the local team and enter fully into the spirit of the occasion. Some of the local car dealers and pubs had big banners placed outside their premises, 'Motherwell for the Cup'. Local bakers had cakes decorated in the Motherwell crest and colours of claret and amber and almost every shop it seemed was adorned with a big Motherwell cup final rosette in the windows. People who had rarely attended a game and in some cases never, excitedly queued up at Fir Park for precious cup final tickets and in the furnace arrangements were made to come in early or swap shifts so that any of the Motherwell fans who wanted to attend the game could do so. Johnny Toolan wasn't to be one of those however. He had briefly considered it but as he hadn't attended any of the other ties he felt he didn't want run the risk of jinxing Motherwell's chances. Of course there was the small matter of the wager as well. Johnny cursed himself for getting involved, he wasn't sure he'd be properly able to enjoy the game because of it but in saying that…..if Motherwell won the cup and he was up to the tune of £200…..ooooft what a day that would be and after all he had given young Ricky Black every opportunity to back away from it. As luck would have it the boys of shift no 2 were backshift when the big day arrived. Those who were working would have to rely on the furnaces being good girls and the big brown Phillips telly in no 1 bothy behaving itself if they were to enjoy the match.

As it turned out the furnaces and the big brown telly were on their best behaviour for the big day so that just about everyone who had wanted to watch the game was able to. Jack took Ricky's stint on the highline so that his friend could watch events unfold in the company of his betting rival Johnny Toolan. Jack missed the first hour of the game as a result but was kept constantly updated on events with shouts from the casting deck below by Harry Badnews and wee Gus. By any standards the 1991 Scottish Cup final proved to be an enthralling classic, fondly remembered by most if not all who saw it to this day.

Motherwell started nervously and United had an early goal disallowed for a narrow offside call, then they hit the inside of the post as the boys in no 1 bothy oohed and aaahed at the frantic start. Gradually though the Lanarkshire side began to settle and Johnny Toolan leapt to his feet as a Griffin cross was met by a flying header into the net by Ferguson. Motherwell held out till half time but early in the second half the Motherwell keeper rose for a cross ball but was clattered by the United centre back and seemed to be in serious discomfort. Had he cracked some ribs? Certainly every move he made seemed to be causing him serious pain. Johnny Toolan hoped he was just winded, playing for time until he got his breath back. Later, however it would emerge he had a lacerated stomach and two broken ribs. Typically, Motherwell were punished as they spurned a chance to play in Arnott and United went straight to the other end and Bowman lashed a shot into the corner for 1-1 leaving Maxwell's broken body prostrate. This all should have handed the initiative to United but incredibly the game swung in the opposite direction. Firstly, 18 year old kid Phil O'Donnell scored his first goal for the club, throwing himself into a flurry of arms, legs and feet to power a diving header into the net and then Angus thundered a shot into the bottom corner for 3-1 as the boys in no 1 bothy and the Motherwell support in the West Stand at Hampden went ballistic! Ricky Black sat in silence seemingly resigned to his fate but this wasn't over yet, not by a long way. That third goal should have tied it up for the 'Well but incredibly this astonishing piece of theatre had more acts to give. With 20 minutes to go O'Neil pulled a goal back for United. With every passing minute the condition of the Motherwell keeper Maxwell seemed to be worsening to the point he was almost immobile at times. Ricky though was infuriated by his antics, considering him as being at it in a bid to waste precious time and for the first time became animated in venting his spleen at the big brown Phillips telly and the unfortunate Maxwell. Johnny Toolan could just tell there would be another twist, there was a reason Motherwell had won fuck all since 1952 and another sting in the tale was coming soon. He was so engrossed in the game all thoughts of the 'wager' had completely gone from his mind. A few feet away Ricky sat pensively stroking the three day old stubble on his face, silently praying for another Dundee United fightback in between bouts of rage at the stricken Maxwell. With seconds remaining the sting in the tail that Johnny Toolan had been waiting on duly arrived, a snapshot of the topsy-turvy nature that defined this incredible Cup final. Arnott broke into a great attacking position for Motherwell, he had two choices, head for the corner to waste time or thread a pass through to the marauding O'Donnell who would surely have the chance to finish the contest. He went for the pass but it didn't find its target and the ball was turned back to the United keeper. Seconds later there was disbelief all round as for the first time Ricky Black was on his feet celebrating to acclaim the United equaliser for 3-3! As soon as he received the ball the United keeper had sent a booming clearance into the Motherwell half and inexplicably the Motherwell defence parted like the Red Sea and Jackson raced through to tower above the prostrate Maxwell and head the bouncing ball home. Ricky sat back down and fingered the bundle of rolled up £10 notes in his pocket excitedly. Maybe he wouldn't have to hand it over after all. 'Sorry wee man' Ricky offered an apology to Johnny for his celebration. 'Naw you're awrite' Johnny laughed, reminded of the bet again for the first time in a while. They smiled briefly at one another aware that there was another 30 minutes of this torture to come as the Cup final went to extra time.

In the few minutes between full time and extra time beginning there was real angst amongst the Motherwell fans within the stadium over the late collapse and how they had seemingly somehow allowed certain victory slip from their grasp. Then there was a sense of everyone galvanising themselves, steeling themselves for what lay ahead and soon the songs began to pour down the stands from the Motherwell end and with renewed optimism at the United end the atmosphere went into overdrive as extra time kicked off. The boys in no 1 bothy could feel the atmosphere crackling through the big brown Phillips telly and both Johnny and Ricky knew that at least another half hour of fraught, nail biting drama was still to come. Jack, fresh from his stint on the highline briefly stood behind the two protagonists of the 'wager' and massaged their shoulders much in the way a trainer might do for a boxer in between rounds. It was a gesture of solidarity to them both as even at this stage Jack genuinely didn't know who to give his support to. He desperately wanted to see the town of Motherwell explode with joy but not at such great expense to his good friend. Over the next thirty minutes it would be his cross to bear alone, the rest of no 1 bothy, young Ricky apart, were firmly in the Motherwell camp.

The main thing about this remarkable spectacle was that you couldn't predict with any certainty which way it was going to go next. Each time one side asserted some control the other would come roaring back. Like two drunken boxers slugging it out till the death. There were plenty punch drunk players running on empty out on the pitch, not least the Motherwell keeper Maxwell. His condition was a real worry for the Motherwell fans and they collectively winced every time the ball went near him. It's at times like these substitutes are vitally important and in Stevie Kirk Motherwell had their own super sub. All the way through the cup run he had stepped up with vital, often stunning goals right out of a 'Roy of the Rovers' annual. A few minutes into extra time he was to prove his worth yet again as a Cooper corner was missed by the United keeper and the ball fell to Kirk. Despite a clutch of United defenders on the line Kirk picked a hole in the white shirted wall and headed the ball through a gap into the net. Cue bedlam in the Motherwell end and amongst the boys in no 1 bothy once more. Again United came roaring back and Jackson fired in a shot that had the stricken Maxwell struggling. Another siege was coming and you just knew that United would get their big chance at some point, the question was could they take it? In the closing minutes they came agonisingly close. First Malpas let fly from distance on a loose ball, the strike seemed to be arcing towards the roof of the net but somehow Maxwell twisted his aching, broken body in the air to flick the ball over the bar. Then as Motherwell struggled to clear the resultant corner the ball fell to Clark but somehow Griffin made a desperate block to force the ball into the side netting. From the angle some United fans were at it must have looked like a goal as they celebrated another last gasp equaliser, but, alas their cheers soon died in their throats as they realised it had gone wide. Finally the referee blew for time and Motherwell players sank to their knees in triumph, the United players in utter devastation. There were celebrations in no 1 bothy as well as Johnny Toolan leapt to his feet and sporadic applause broke out amongst some of the other lads. Johnny turned towards young Ricky. He was just about to tell him to keep his money in his pocket when Ricky pressed the bundle of notes into his hand and gave him an awkward embrace. 'Fair play wee man, yeez deserved it, some game', he said. With that Ricky turned and fled for his stint on the highline, leaving no chance of further debate. Johnny thought about following him and trying to give him the money back but he knew it was hopeless. A bet was a bet and always pay your dues. Simple rules to live your life by. Jack thought about following his friend out as well and offering his condolences, he felt for him and deplored the curse of his luckless gambling madness, but he would wait a while and give his friend some time to get over it. Maybe he'd be up for a pint later and Jack would stand him a drink or two after his loss, it was the least he could do. Jack wondered with excitement what the town of Motherwell's cup final party would look like and resolved to have a look for himself at finishing time.

If Jack had any concerns that two hours spent watching £200 disappear down the drain would dampen Ricky's enthusiasm for joining the Motherwell party, he needn't have worried. By the time Jack went up to the highline to relieve his friend for the last hour of the shift, Ricky's affable, easy going demeanour was back in evidence. 'You alright?' Jack enquired. 'Aye sound mate, whit's fur ye'll no go by ye, eh?' came the standard reply. 'You up tae coming tae join the party? I can sub ye if yer a bit light after today', suggested Jack. 'Na, am fine mate. I'm up for joining the celebrations. Why not, eh? We'll cadge a lift down tae Motherwell aff wee Gus and join the party if ye like', Ricky offered. 'Sounds like a plan', said Jack and the preparations for the night ahead were set.

One thing about pulling a shift on the highline if you were heading straight out for a night out was that you would need to pay that bit extra attention in the showers afterwards. The highline, perched high in the air, was a series of belts feeding the raw materials to the hoppers down below before being despatched in the desired weight into skips via the scale car or a series of filter screens then up to the top of the furnace to be tipped into the big melting pot. A cold wet day up there, apart from being fucking freezing meant that all the dust from the coke or sinter or ore stuck to everything and you'd inevitably spend half the time choking huddled over a frost fire. Guard rails, belts, levers, the lot were coated in dust. Worse still, was a dry summers day like today when the dust was ten times worse and billowed and spread out like smoke hanging in the air. It got everywhere and I mean everywhere. Into all the folds and lines on your skin, in the tear ducts of your eyes and deep inside your ears. It wouldn't have been the first time Ricky or Jack had been asked on a night out if they were wearing eyeliner or mascara, having to explain about the dust on the job whilst standing there looking like a fuckin extra out of Duran Duran! So it was with due care and attention that the lads took to the showers on this fine Saturday evening.

By the time they reached town the party of a lifetime was in full swing. It was a release for the town from the constant campaigning to 'save the 'Craig' or 'save our steel', the constant speculation of when the axe might fall on the big plant and what effect it might have. The streets were thronged with happy drinkers and there were Motherwell colours everywhere. A street vendor was making a killing selling scarves, flags and hats and

Jack and Ricky bought one each to get into the spirit of it all. Every pub from the Horse Shoe at the cross right up the Cross Keys in Wishaw was jam packed as the towns of Motherwell and Wishaw acclaimed Motherwell's remarkable victory. One of the pubs was even selling pints at 1952 prices (the last time Motherwell had won the cup) and Jack and Ricky tried to squeeze their way in but to no avail. In the end they joined the queue to get into Faces nightclub and danced and sang and drank the rest of the night away with the rest of the happy crowd. What a day it had been and what a night it was, in fact you'd be hard pushed to find anyone who was sober enough to remember much of the evening's frivolity in the town. It was a day when heroes became legends. Ally Maxwell, Luc Nijholt, Craig Paterson, Chris McCart, Tam Boyd, Jim Griffin, Ian Angus, Phil O'Donnell, Davie Cooper, Ian Ferguson, Dougie Arnott, Stevie Kirk and Colin O'Neil had written themselves into folklore. It was also a day that saw Ricky Black further enhance his reputation as the unluckiest gambler on shift no 2!

THE AXE FALLS

Death by a thousand cuts they had called it. The first clear sign that British Steel were fully intent on the closure of Ravenscraig was the closure of the rolling mill at Gartcosh in 1986. Everyone knew from then that it was only a matter of time. Sure there were the campaigns and 'Save our Steel' and 'Save the Craig' stickers adorned most if not all the shop windows in the area and the community came together as one to try and stave off the inevitable. The tabloids jostled for position as the Sun and the Record battled to be the voice of the people. There were the protest meetings and marches. ISTC union chief Tommy Brennan, a man of great principle helped drive the campaigns and worked tirelessly on the workers behalf. There was lobbying of politicians too, questions asked in parliament. A compelling case was built structured around the way the workforce had adapted to changing market conditions, new techniques and embracing new technology to confound the critics and produce the best quality steel in the world. But market forces was the mantra of the Conservative government and everyone knew that there was no way of competing on price with the cheap imports from China and elsewhere. There was a brief ray of hope when the furnaces at Ravenscraig were selected to trial new cutting edge technology in the shape of a new coal injection plant designed to improve efficiency. Any hope though that this new plant would provide a stay of execution was swiftly taken away however when the lads saw how it was constructed. It was basically a giant meccano set on stilts, connected to the furnace by a myriad of flexi hoses and tubes, easily deconstructed and shipped off to elsewhere. 'It'll be on a fuckin lorry down tae Wales in a few months' was the popular cry from some of the lads. No, there was to be no stay of execution and in fact in January 1992 after reducing to a one furnace operation the previous year British Steel plc reneged on their previously stated promise to maintain the plant until at least 1994........and announced its closure in September later that year. Everyone had seen it coming but there had been so many false dawns and scare stories that it still came as a shock. It was finally over………..the axe had fallen!

One by one the boys of shift no2 were called up to the security block at the main gate to receive their redundancy offers. When it came to his turn Jack took his letter into the room provided and sat down shaking with trepidation and fiddled with the large A4 envelope in his hands. There had been much speculation as to who would get what amongst the shift and when someone on the admin side of things leaked some of the details of the formula they were using, most of the lads had been able to calculate broadly what to expect from the paperwork now in Jack's hands. To see the confirmation of it in black and white though, that was quite something else. There was a covering letter that explained what was happening in terms of the closure. Overleaf there was a breakdown of the terms of the redundancy payment, the details of niceties like tax and national insurance, how to calculate what lieu of notice was due and a formula was provided to allow you to check the figures of the offer. Jack scanned these two pages and cut to the chase turning over to the main event. There he saw it in pounds and pence, what his job was worth to British Steel, the axeman Black Bob Scholley and all the fuckin rest like the Tories who had been complicit in the closure. Jack let out a low whistle at sight of the figure. He knew that he was luckier than many who didn't get the luxury of the big cheque when they lost their livelihood but that didn't make any of this any easier. That initial moment of euphoria was then lost as Jack quickly calculated that the figure proposed was just over a years wages and he began to wonder if he would be sorted with another job by the time that year had passed. Surely, he thought, but doing what? All of the lads had been putting the feelers out for work already but few had any joy in terms of setting anything up and there were precious few firms who could match the wages they were currently on. Jack began turning all of this over in his mind and as he traipsed back towards the furnace the euphoria and excitement had been replaced with anxiety and his head was in a spin with so many questions over the future for which he had no answers.

In the great tradition of the steelmen socialising with one another, a farewell do was arranged for the final shift, the final cast had been made and a skeleton crew stayed on to complete the rundown of both furnaces. It would take several months of careful planning and decommissioning to finally close the chapter, it wasn't just a case of padlocking the gates and saying cheerio. In fact it would be many years before the land was reclaimed and deep suspicions remained over toxins lying deep underground, an unwanted souvenir of almost forty years of steelmaking. The vast majority of the men including Jack and Ricky had been given their date for finishing and as luck would have it their stint as 'G' men in the blast furnace would finally end on a Friday dayshift with the rest of the lads of shift no 2. A farewell party was organised in the ex-servicemans club and a band booked and of course they would have all day to build up to it saying their fond farewells to Mary in the Era bar and the boys behind the bar in the King Lud. It was one of several dos arranged over the weekend and the ISTC rep Tommy Brennan encouraged the men all to attend and celebrate their achievements together and reminisce over the old days and just as importantly celebrate each other, embracing the future together.

Ricky had surprised Jack on that day by dipping out of the pre-drinks party before the big do at the ex-serviceman's club. 'I've got something I have to do big man, I'll catch up with everyone later' he had said. Jack remembered wondering what could be more important than the last shift and the farewell do or wake as some had called it but he figured it must have been important to his friend and that was good enough for him. Maybe he was chasing down a lead on a new job opportunity? The rest of the crew trooped out of the Craigneuk gate for one last time, Jack, Harry, wee Rab, Tommy Wilson, the Chief, Gus and Jake. Harry Badnews stopped and turned to look back at the big blue cooling tower, for so long the beacon of the areas industrial strength. Jack noticed and stopped with him and saw his eyes begin to fill with tears. 'Am awful sorry son', said Harry as the pair locked eyes together. 'Whit fur?' replied Jack genuinely puzzled. 'Going on about that horse, yon fuckin Media Star Guest. I knew ye felt bad about it but I just wouldnae stop ribbing ye about it. Sorry son.' Jack smiled at the mention of that crazy fuckin horse that had a mind of its own. 'That's alright Harry, it wisnae ma finest hour anyway', replied Jack and with that he gently took Harry by the shoulders and spun him around throwing an arm around his shoulder. 'Come on mate, don't look back, only forwards now. It'll be alright. Whit's fur ye'll no go by ye. We're big rugged ironworkers mind, nothings gonnae keep us down' and with that they made to catch up with the others heading for the Era bar. 'Come on Harry that you trying tae dodge the first round as usual?' called back Tommy Wilson.

Across the Clyde and a few miles away in Larkhall, Pamela Martin was ironing her uniform for the afternoon shift at the hospital. Pamela was aware it was a big day for Ricky and all the steelmen, the axe had finally fallen and like the hard drinking working class men they were, there would have to be the big send off to bring the curtain down on an iconic workplace that had served the whole of the Lanarkshire area in different ways for generations. There were the newsagents that sold them their rolls and papers, the bookies that took their betting lines, the pubs that served them their pints, the small independent traders who sold them their carpets and furnishings, the travel agents that sold them their holidays and the fashion retailers who clothed them, not-withstanding the long list of contractors who had direct business with the 'Craig. Yes, this was a momentous day for the area for sure and many more than just the steelworkers themselves wondered about how the wolf would be kept from the door. Pamela was wondering when she might see Ricky and what state he might be in later when she was suddenly startled to hear a key turning in the front door of her flat. To her surprise in walked Ricky. She was just about to ask what he was doing home when he marched over to her and buried his face on her shoulder and began to sob uncontrollably. 'Whatever's the matter?' she soothed. She could barely get any sense out of him for a few minutes but then gradually he began to calm down. When he did it transpired that Ricky was devastated about today. Devastated about losing his friends, his way of life and terrified about what might lie in the future. He was adamant he wasn't going to the big party at the ex-serviceman's club, 'Can't face it ', he said. Gradually Pamela talked him round. He couldn't let the boys down today of all days, after all, they were all in it together. As for the future, that would sort itself out and they would face it together. 'Now go and get a shower and I'll make you something to eat', she ordered. Ricky felt better, calmer. He could always rely on Pamela to right him when he felt as though he'd been turned upside down. She was right, he couldn't let the boys down today, especially Jack. He would go and get a shower, have something to eat then go and join the fray such as it was. As for the future, it would be alright. 'Whit's fur ye'll no go by ye.'

Jack had been eyeing the door anxiously for a time, scanning the entrance for Ricky but gradually as the numerous pints he had downed began to take hold he began to relax. He needn't have worried anyway as just as the band began to set up his friend arrived. No one was quite sure who had booked and organised the evening's events but they had done a grand job for sure. The band took the assembled throng on a journey through the classics, from the Beatles to the Stones and the Eagles. Pretty soon the lads were belting out familiar songs together like 'Love Is In The Air' and 'Sweet Caroline'. After a time the band began to invite singers on stage to join them and there was no shortage of takers. Emboldened by his alcohol intake Jack decided to regale the crowd with his rendition of American Pie. Davie Kellacher had taught him the song one night in the furnace at New Year when they'd both landed a nightshift at Hogmanay. It was one of those unwritten rules that the young single guys would cover the Christmas holiday period for the guys with families. Jack went down a storm and pretty soon everyone was up on their feet joining in with the song, it was almost as if he had caught the mood. There were a couple of moments when he struggled to remember the words but the band stepped in and covered his forgetfulness and got him going again. When he stepped off the stage he was greeted by a standing ovation and there was much backslapping when he returned to his table. 'Aw these years and we didnae know you could sing big yin' roared Johnny Toolan as the Chief wrapped him up in a bear hug. Jack looked across and saw Ricky laughing over giving him the thumbs up, it felt good. There was an anxious moment later when the band belted out the Rangers anthem 'Simply The Best' but the Celtic fans amongst the crowd joined in with it and when the band played the Celtic anthem 'You'll Never Walk Alone' a little later Rangers fans reciprocated, well, all apart from big DC Paterson of course who sat glumly with his arms folded. But there would be no old firm bitterness to spoil this night, no chance. All too soon, as the evening began to wind down Ricky bounded over to Jack. 'Come on big man, we going to check out one of these night clubs before they're all shut fuckin down?' he implored. Actually Ricky was far more accurate with his assertion than he might have realised. Pretty soon most of the clubs were gone. Some closed very quickly, seeing the writing on the wall, others died a slow lingering death as they held out in the misplaced hope of an unlikely new dawn. As it was, as they reminisced over what had gone before and wondered what might befall them in the future, Ricky and Jack ended that night propping one another up on the dancefloor of Faces nightclub belting out the Whitney Houston song 'Didn't We Almost Have It All'. The ride with you was worth the fall my friend, didn't we almost have it all.

EPILOGUE

RICKY BLACK

It's fair to say that Ricky Black struggled in aftermath of the closure of Ravenscraig. Riddled with uncertainty and indecision over where his future lay and unsure of his place in this new world he drifted along aimlessly battling with the romantic notion he had of himself and his past. The DTI (Department of Trade and Industry) sponsored training courses and make up money were a godsend during this period. Basically, for redundant steelworkers, this Government scheme was designed to ease people back into work by making up your wage from any job you were able to get up to levels comparable with your rate of pay at Ravenscraig. After all there were few employers paying anything like the money the boys were used to at that time. Similarly, if you embarked on an approved training course the DTI would sustain your wage for up to 50 weeks. It was a way of cushioning the blow and of delaying the inevitable moment when you would have to dip your toes into the icy cold waters of the Tories free market. All the lads were encouraged to do re-training of some kind if they couldn't find work and there were few who could afford to look this gift horse in the mouth and walk the other way.

Ricky marvelled at the array of training options on offer, but what the fuck could you do in a year that would guarantee a job at the end? Most decent courses with qualifications worth having were for at least 3 or 4 years. Ricky thought he had discovered the answer when he bumped into Gerry Bonner in Hamilton one day. One of the colleges were offering the ASME IX coded pipe welding course, Gerry advised. Initially they would train you from the basics up, depending on your skillset, on all aspects of welding and then at the end of the year you would sit the coded pipe welding test. If you passed there were jobs aplenty for decent money in Holland and elsewhere. 'Sounds fuckin ideal' thought Ricky and signed up the very next day not forgetting to send his forms off to the DTI for the make up money. When he embarked on the course which was at Motherwell College there were a clutch of other keen ex-steelworkers there ready to embark on a new chapter in their working lives. As they passed each other the paperwork they had to fill in the banter was flying around and Ricky even recognised one or two faces from the finishing end and the maintenance crews. This was gonnae be a good laugh, just like old times thought Ricky. There was just one problem. Welding was hard, especially welding a pipe trying to keep a 45 degree angle all the way round the fucking thing and Ricky soon discovered he was absolutely hopeless at it. You needed a steady hand and a keen eye and Ricky had neither. It was almost an art form and Ricky marvelled at the workmanship of the instructors and some of the lads to be fair, as they weaved little waves and metallic beads of perfect fusion around two great chunks of pipe. In comparison his welds were skinny uneven looking things like a line of untidy ants following each other round the merry go round. He was constantly either blowing a hole right through the pipe or getting the welding rod stuck on it, then getting eye-flash as threw his visor up in frustration and yanked at it to try and free it. Then would come the expletives from behind his curtained booth as he cursed 'the fuckin, bastard, cunting thing!' Some of the other lads were actual welders, just on the course for the make up money then off to wherever with the qualification. They were patient with the greenhorns like Ricky and tried to help them as best they could, even letting the boys pass off some of their work as their own as they went through the different modules. In Ricky's case it was hopeless though. He was no good at this and after trying to make a fist of it of it for a few months he was making enquiries on switching courses. He took to playing hooky as well, heading down to the Fir Park Club for lunch and staying there the rest of the afternoon, sinking the amber nectar to ease his troubles.

Eventually Ricky switched onto a logistics course but within a few days he realised he'd fucked up again. He couldn't make head nor tail of what they were talking about half the time and after another illuminating chat with Gerry Bonner he switched again onto a painting and decorating course. As Gerry had told him, the instructor didn't give a fuck. Once you had signed in and all the 'i's' dotted and the 't's crossed you could do what you wanted. In the morning they would make for the college canteen for breakfast and eye up all the birds over a few hands of cards. Then it was down to the Fir Park Club or Jack Daniels for lunch and a few frames of pool or snooker. Ricky spent the rest of his 50 weeks soaking up the Tenents Lager from the tap at the bar as he tried to push thoughts of his bleak outlook to the back of his mind.

Pamela Martin knew that the closure of the 'Craig had hit Ricky hard. In fact she had known things weren't right with him since long before then. She knew him better than anyone and could see past that 'whit's fur ye'll no go by ye' bravado that he fronted up for everyone else. She watched him struggle with the darkness inside him and the self-doubt as he frittered away the 50 weeks of make up money and the training opportunity afforded to him. After the training period was over it was time to get a job but Ricky couldn't stick to anything. He got the sack from Motorola over his timekeeping, or so he had told Pamela, but in truth it was over the way he had blown up about it when his supervisor had challenged him on it. His timekeeping had never been a problem before, after all he'd been a good neebur in the 'Craig. He just couldn't motivate himself to go to that fuckin place. He hated its sterile environment and the whole American corporate business ethic it had espoused. Fuck, one of the questions at the interview had been 'What would you do if you saw someone stealing mobile phones from the shop floor?' He had said that he didn't know but hoped he'd do the right thing but he knew what they were looking for......a fuckin grass. His answer must have been good enough for the smiley cow that interviewed him though, for he got the job, although not for long.

After he got the tin tack from Motorola he spent weeks looking for something else and eventually landed a gig at a distribution warehouse. He hated that as well. It was fuckin freezing in that place most of the time and all the others on his 'team' were fuckin weirdos that he couldn't take to at all. After just a couple of months in there a drop off in the firm's order book meant they had to cut back some jobs. It was suggested to him that if he made his case to his supervisor he wouldn't be amongst those on the list for the chop. Apparently he was well thought of by the snooty cow in question. Ricky never bothered going to see her though, fuck that! It was a relief to him when the list of those being paid off came round and his name was on it. After that it took him months to find something else. In truth he hadn't been trying too hard, hating the weekly visits to the jobcentre, standing in line with the unemployed and unemployable. Eventually though he pressed on and made a sustained effort to land something as the guilt over the extra shifts Pamela was having to pull to keep them afloat kicked his arse into gear. He landed a packing job at a plastics warehouse on constant nightshift. With the shift allowance added in the wage was just about bearable but the job itself was a fuckin nightmare, a living hell. A lot of the other packers were agency workers and when they didn't show up for work as was often the case, you had to cover the other machines. You could spend all night running back and forth chasing your fuckin tail and the only concession was you could switch the machines off for half an hours break. One night with moulds piling up all around him Ricky walked off the job and never went back. 'They can find some other fuckin mug', Ricky mouthed over his shoulder as one of his co-workers asked what he was doing.

All the while Pamela remained patient with him but it was getting harder and harder. With her medical background she had realised that he was most likely in the grip of some kind of depression but getting him to admit it and ask for help was another matter entirely. They'd had conversations about it when she'd encouraged him to open up. Depression was an illness just like any other and left untreated it would only get worse she had told him. But naw, fuck that! He wasn't some lunatic for the funny farm and in need of happy pills to get through the day. He'd laugh it off like always and they'd pretend everything would be alright but a day of reckoning would come some day and Pamela knew it. After the nightshift job was lost Ricky sank ever deeper into the black hole he was in and what's worse he was beginning to drag Pamela in there with him. She had been his rock. She had been there for him all along the way. She had raised his spirits when he was down, soothed him when he felt at his darkest and more than that, she had kept them afloat. She took extra shifts at the hospital whenever she could and even took on some shifts on at her Dad's social club the Lea Rig. All her family liked Ricky and his easy going nature but they could all see what was happening. He was pissing his life away, drowning in a sea of darkness and he was taking Pamela down with him. Words had been said and although Pamela would defend him to the hilt to others she knew that something would have to be done. It was one night when she came home off a backshift and saw him lying there, sleeping the sleep of the half pissed, a soft mound of flesh protruding from under his t shirt and between his waist band where his taut stomach had once been, that she realised that the time had come. Time for some home truths, time to lay it on the line for him once and for all. She looked at him sadly and wondered where the boy she had fallen in love with had gone. Oh, he was still in there somewhere, she was sure of that, there were still enough occasional glimpses of him but they were becoming more and more fleeting. She wasn't giving up on him but she would talk to him in the morning and this time the outcome would have to be different.

To Pamela's surprise she found Ricky to be far more receptive to her harsh words than she had imagined. It was almost as though he had come to the realisation himself that he had reached a fork in the road. As he looked at himself in the mirror sadly, he saw himself as Pamela did. The hooded eyes, the puffed up cheeks and the beginnings of the beer belly he had sworn he would never succumb to. It was time to choose his destiny. She soothed his worries about speaking to a doctor and taking the happy pills. She would be with him every step of the way and they would get through this together like they always did. She booked an appointment for that very afternoon and Ricky began to take the first fragile steps to recovery.

There was no noticeable change for a while, although with Pamela's encouragement Ricky did cut back on the boozing and the gambling although the sight of the beer belly staring back at him in the mirror every morning and a lack of cash probably played at least as big a part in these developments as anything else. He began to get active again as well, playing the odd game of fives and getting back to the swimming baths and the gym. It was tentative at first but then as he began to feel better he became more proactive. Then the darkness that was inside him gradually began to trickle out. Like an oil tanker holed below the water line it dribbled out at first then all at once it surged out of him gushing out in a flood of tears and regret. He told Pamela of how he had watched Benny Cleland take his last breath in the coke ovens, of the day the ambulances came for them when they had been gassed at no 1 furnace, of old Jimmy Morton's screams the day he stepped into a puddle of slag metal, of his feelings of insecurity, of never being good enough. Not good enough for her nor good enough to live up to the reputation he'd earned as the easy going good guy with that 'whit's fur ye'll no go by ye' take on life. Pamela held him and soothed him as it all poured out of him in inglorious technicolour and at last she began to understand some of what had been going on in his head all these years. Finally, she knew what the nightmares he had were all about and promised to help him cast them out for good.

Sometimes it's not about what you know, but who you know as the saying goes. Throughout Ricky's struggles Pamela had a friend always happy to lend an ear in her cousin Mhairi. As Ricky began the road to recovery Pamela began to regale Mhairi with the tales of horror and tragedy Ricky had told her from his days in the 'Craig. She did so partly in the therapeutic way of needing to share and also by way of explanation for some of Ricky's behaviour over the last couple of years. Mhairi and her husband Martin had been good friends of the couple and they'd often all make up a fun foursome on nights out but as Ricky had entered his downward spiral Martin began to put some distance between him and Ricky. He had suspected that a combination of the big redundancy pay out Ricky had received and an unhealthy dose of self- pity were at the root of his troubles. So when Mhairi began to relay the tales of what the lad had been going through, Martin, not unnaturally began to feel a little guilty. He'd always really liked Ricky but felt perhaps he had abandoned him just when he needed help the most. Upon seeing Ricky's apparent fightback for himself one day over a pint and a few frames of pool in the Electric Bar, Martin resolved to help the lad any way he could. As luck would have it the bottling plant where Martin was a shift manager were in need of a technician. A word in the right ear and Ricky had an interview arranged for the very next week.

Although Ricky Blacks battle with depression would never be completely over its fair to say that the day he was offered the job in the bottling plant in Glasgow was the day when he won the war. He threw himself into this new beginning with enthusiasm. He enjoyed the work and began to make new friends very quickly. He even enjoyed the morning commute into Glasgow on the train, watching the 9 to 5 office crowd, the guys suited and booted and the girls with their tailored jackets and skirts, chatting excitedly about their weekend or their plans for the next one. After just a few months he gained a promotion to shift supervisor as well, as his hard work ethic and likeability began to shine through. It's just as well that promotion came through as well what with another mouth to feed soon, for Pamela had fallen pregnant and Ricky Black would soon be a father.

Although the battle with the darkness and self-doubt within him was ongoing Ricky was almost back to being himself again and Pamela for one was overjoyed to see it and couldn't wait for their family to be complete. But Ricky knew he wasn't the same person any more, no. No more 'whit's fur ye'll no go by ye', for him. You make your own luck in this world and Ricky Black was determined to make his all it could be, not just for him but for Pamela as well and the unborn child living inside her. Ricky doesn't see many of the boys from the 'Craig around these days, apart from Jack. Come to think of it, he hadn't seen his big buddy Jack for a long while either. 'Really must give him a call soon', thought Ricky as he strode confidently through the gates to another shift at the bottling plant.

JACK LEONARD

Every cloud has a silver lining and all that and although for most, in the end of steelmaking at the 'Craig it was hard to see one, for Jack Leonard the arrival of the big cheque provided a solution to one thorny problem. In short, it was a game changer. Jack had long since known he had wanted to pop the question to his beloved Rachel but every time he had raised the subject Rachel's expression would change and she would shut down on him. Rachel's parents had divorced when she was a teenager and the split had been acrimonious pitching a family at war with each other. It was a rift where battle lines had long since been drawn and those unwilling to pick a side like Rachel and Jack had to tread carefully. A family wedding and indeed the build up to it would simply become the breeding ground for settling old scores and re-hashing old arguments and Rachel had no desire to be the centrepiece of it. It was bad enough her sister had to escape to London and marry quietly in a registry office to avoid the madness. Jack had broached the subject of them doing similar but after turning the possibility over in her mind for a while Rachel had dismissed the notion. She may not have wanted a big family do but she wanted it to be special and sloping off to some registry office on the quiet wasn't for her. Still, Jack had thought he had planted some sort of seed at last and he seized on her hesitation.

One night after Brookside, Jack watched a programme on channel 4 about couples booking holiday wedding packages in the Caribbean and thought immediately he just might have stumbled upon the answer. Surely if he presented the idea to Rachel properly, made it special, a proposal wrapped in the allure of a Caribbean escape she wouldn't be able to resist? Jack set his plan in motion and visited the local travel agent A.T. Mays to make enquiries. Sure enough they had a wedding specialist who took care of every detail from the dress, the flowers, the photographer and even the witnesses if required. Jack made a provisional booking and set about planning his proposal, after all he was going to have to make this irresistible, he wasn't quite sure he could contemplate what road they would go down if Rachel turned him down. He knew it would take a fair chunk out of the redundancy money but he didn't care and figured every penny would be worth it if it set them on their way to a lifetime together.

One Friday night when an unsuspecting Rachel came home from work he met her at the door of their flat. He had a huge bouquet of red and white roses waiting for her, there was champagne on ice, none of your cheap Brut shite out of Asda but a bottle of Laurent Perrier blush. He had made up a mixed tape of her favourite songs from her favourite artists and had it playing softly in the background. Tunes from the likes of Alison Moyet, The Beautiful South and Hue and Cry provided a musical backdrop to the big moment. 'What's all this?' Rachel asked adding 'oh my God' as Jack went down on one knee and popped open the box containing the sapphire engagement ring he had on approval from Beaverbrooks. He saw the look of foreboding begin to creep across Rachel's expression as he said the words, 'will you marry me?' 'Jack, we've talked about this', she said, her hands shaking as she stared open mouthed at the ring. Before she could say any more Jack sprung to his feet and hurriedly told her of his Caribbean escape plan. Gradually, Rachel's face began to lighten as she listened and after what seemed like an eternity she let loose with a gentle sigh and then she said it. 'Okay, yes, let's do it.' The pair hugged one another tightly pausing only to put the ring on her finger, it was a little tight and she'd have to get it sized but nothing was going to spoil their happiness tonight and the family at war could all go fuck themselves. Jack and Rachel would be married in just 6 weeks' time and on the white sands near Montego Bay they would take their vows to each other and begin their journey together as man and wife.

Like Ricky, Jack had been made aware of the apparently easy route into a new career in the shape of the ASME IX welding course, via of course from the font of all knowledge of such things, a certain Mr. Gerry Bonner. However as a firm believer in that old adage that if something looked too good to be true then it probably was, he was somewhat sceptical. Anyway he had just spent years sweating his bollocks off, inhaling fumes from a dusty industrial environment and had no desire for his next career choice to take him down a similar route. Heavy industry was dying on its arse Jack reasoned and computers were the future and the way forward for a young man like himself. He'd seen it first hand in the 'Craig as the new technology had crept in and become increasingly prevalent. Under Thatcher and then Major this new white collar industry was thriving as the old ones died out. That was Jack's thinking as he debated which route was the best to take with the 50 weeks of DTI sponsored training he was entitled to. Sure, it was tempting to join Ricky and Gerry and some of the others who he knew that had signed up for the welding course. It would be a great laugh and a comfort to be with familiar faces as they tried to carve out a new start together, but the future lay elsewhere, Jack was sure of that much and so, with the encouragement of Rachel and others whose opinion he valued he signed up for a computer course at the Bell College in Hamilton.

Jack was initially impressed with his new pristine surroundings. He liked the clean lines of the college, the chatter in the corridors and in the canteen, everyone sporting the best look they could muster with no need for airstream helmets, visors, RFD boots, welder's gloves or donkey jackets. In his class there was only one former steelworker, a guy called Davie Francis. Davie had worked in the slab yard down at the finishing end of the 'Craig and Jack thought he vaguely recognised him at first. He seemed like a nice enough guy but Jack was ill at ease around him. He had this way of holding eye contact with you and then maintaining it for a time after a conversation had clearly ended that disturbed Jack a bit. He just seemed to be so intense. They had gone for a drink together after an early finish at the college one Friday afternoon and done the rounds of a few of the pubs in the Peacock Cross area near the Bell. Rather than relax the bold Davie the drink just seemed to make him even more intense than usual. He became particularly animated when talking about his penchant for martial arts, twisting Jack's arm up his back as he demonstrated some fuckin Kung Fu move or other. By the time the afternoon's frivolity had come to an end Jack had come to the conclusion that (a) he had nothing in common with Davie Francis, (b) Davie Francis was de facto, a fuckin weirdo and (c) Davie Francis couldn't hold his drink. All things considered it wasn't an experience to be repeated and Jack vowed to give the daft cunt a wide berth in future.

Another new development Jack had to deal with was the presence of women in his class. Jack had never worked with women before and in his entire working life had only really come across them as middle aged ladies in the canteen at the 'Craig. There had been one day when a girl appeared up on deck at the furnaces with the geek squad, apparently she had been an engineering student on a placement. Jack remembered with a smile what a stir this attractive blond in a donkey jacket had caused and laughed at the memory of the lads on the shift all huddled round the CCTV to get a look at her, some of the lads had even made random excuses to leave their posts just to get a look at this curious sight. In truth though that was about the entire extent of Jack's experience of women in the workplace! There were a few in his class, some of them attractive as well and for a time Jack was uncertain around them, unsure of how the easy but crass working man's banter of the 'Craig would sit with them, unsure of where the new boundaries would lie and for a while it made him a little insular and insecure. Gradually he began to relax into this new social scene though even allowing himself to indulge in some occasionally flirtatious banter with some of the girls. In the main though he made sure to keep the chat light and professional, aware that for most this course was a means to an end and nothing more. One girl in particular however, a striking brunette named Leeanne, had made it pretty clear that she was keen on Jack but he kept her at arms-length, making sure he dropped Rachel into the conversation whenever possible. Jack and Rachel had moved into a rented flat in Burnbank together in the run up to the closure of the 'Craig. With her steady job in the court and nearly a year of DTI money to come, in a sense the pressure was off them, but the anxiety of what was to come next was always prevalent and over the coming months would grow.

Fairly early on into his course Jack began to realise that the qualification he would earn would only give him a basic grounding in the subject. Yes it would be an asset in terms of applying for some jobs but as a gateway into the industry itself he would need at least another year's study, possibly two more, to have any hope of gaining a shot at something more meaningful. The work itself was okay and Jack passed all the various modules required without too much difficulty but he found it monotonous and mind crushingly dull. Long before the end of the 50 weeks Jack began to fret that he'd made a mistake and began to test the waters outside applying for every job that looked attainable. The 'thanks, but no thanks' letters began to pile up with alarming regularity and Jack's anxiety that there might not be anything at all out there for him increased as the end of the training period drew ever closer.

Jack's first visit to the cashline machine after the last of the make up money had been paid out brought home the stark reality as the balance figure on the readout stared at him accusingly. Jack would need to scale down his expectations and get a job, any fuckin job. In desperation he applied for a private hire taxi badge. He knew some of the lads in the 'Craig had used their redundancy money to put taxis on the road and had met one of them in the street a few weeks before. Phil Cotter had been the scale car driver on shift no 3 and he and young Jack had bonded easily over a shared love of Celtic F.C. Phil had told Jack that if he ever needed a few shifts driving to give him a call and also told him how easy it was to get your badge. Fifty quid and a few forms to fill in seemed like an easy way to gain access to earning a living but as with all things in life there's a price to pay somewhere. Jack was to learn that price over the coming weeks as he discovered that taxi drivers don't earn their crust all that easily. First there was the weigh in, the fifty quid a week radio money to be paid to the operator before you'd earned a coin.

Then there were the punters, oh Jesus some of those punters! The firm Cotter's taxis were attached to had Castlemilk and Rutherglen as their catchment area, two hardy, working class areas in the South East of Glasgow. Jack had his eyes opened on the very first day as he picked up two junkies in Rutherglen bound for Possilpark to score their hit for the day. 'Ah, a new guy', said the sandy haired one his gaunt features peering at Jack through the window, 'Ah'll tell ye how it works big man,' he added. Apparently this was a daily run, twenty quid paid up front, a wee stop at the shop in Polmadie for supplies, fags and irn bru and a bag full of Mueller fruit corners which bizarrely, were seemingly the food of choice for your average Glasgow junkie. Then it was on to Possilpark, a sprawling den of a housing scheme to the north of the town to score a hit. Jack was asked to park on a side street and wait as the pair dashed off to make their deal. He heard the sandy haired one give off a loud whistle, some sort of signal he figured and within less than five minutes the pair were back in the car having secured themselves another little bag of oblivion. On the way back they asked Jack if he wanted to buy a fireplace. The big furniture warehouse near Shawfield had been raided the week before and although the addicts in the rear of Jack's taxi didn't own up to responsibility for it they went into great detail about how the job had been done and with a wink added that they could get Jack a good price......'best ae gear', they assured him. Jack marvelled at how they could afford this expense on a daily basis. 'Full time fuckin job this lark', the sandy haired one explained. Before they left the taxi and were ensconced back at their flat in Rutherglen they handed Jack a pack of twenty Club Kingsize by way of a tip. Jack had been trying to give up the fags for the last few months. Hardly anyone had smoked at the college apart from the ever hopeful Leeanne following him out for a conspiratorial smoke, but Jack took the packet from them. He figured he was probably going to need a wee smoke now and then on this job!

In truth the junkies were probably amongst Jack's best punters and he made the same trip three times over the next ten days, same routine every time. On the last trip though the pair had become embroiled in an argument over money on the way home. Just as Jack pulled onto their street they started a full on fight in the back of the car, punching utter fuck out of each other. To be fair to them they took it outside as soon he pulled up at the flats secure entry door, but Jack vowed to make it his last trip with them, he'd seen quite enough of the junkie run to Possil thank you very much! Almost as bad as the junkies were the old dears with their bags of shopping. No harm to them but the time wasted, fetching and carrying and helping them in and out of the car, all for a fuckin poxy two quid fare at the end of it wasn't going to pay the bills. He used to sigh every time he pulled into the Mitchell Arcade and saw some poor old soak standing there leaning on a trolley load of bags. He always remained polite and helpful though, remembering the Chief's wise words 'you'll be an auld man yirself wan day son.' All the same it was hard to remain patient sometimes especially when you'd just done a cash count and you were nowhere near your target.

If the old dears were a pain, the drunks at night were worse, especially groups of young lads. You could smell the alcohol as soon as the door opened, the odour of stale beer or whisky or wine hitting you in the face as if a stark reminder of what life had become. Some of them were fine, cracking jokes, full of the banter, but on more than few occasions there was the unmistakable air of menace as you were warned to take the right route or 'better no be fuckin rippin us off here driver or yar fuckin jaw'll get ripped!' Why did the widest cunt, the biggest smart arse always have to sit in the seat behind the driver so you couldn't see what was going on? One night after having been given one such warning Jack gulped as he saw the unmistakable flash of steel in the rear view mirror, a menacing glare as the punter ran his finger across the blade, this job was fast becoming Jack's biggest nightmare. The final straw came one Friday night as Jack dropped a young couple off in town. He envied them cuddling up to one another in the back seat before they set off into the Glasgow night for dinner and a few drinks. He was just about to head back for Castlemilk when a call came in for a hire just a couple of streets away dropping off in his area anyway. As

Jack slowed down he saw his prospective hire, a tall blond girl wearing a very short skirt and tottering in high heels towards him, her arm outstretched to flag him down. Jack noticed a hint of stocking top under her skirt as she came closer and he felt a sudden stirring in his loins. Phwwoooah, what the fuckin hell was he getting here? Any rush of libido soon disappeared however as the interior light clicked on in the back to reveal the sunken eyes, gaunt features and haunted look of yet another Glasgow junkie. Jack's cock virtually disappeared up his own arse as the gravelly voice in the back instructed him to take her to 'Castlemilk mate, Dougrie Drive.' Jack didn't bother with any chit chat after that, in fact he turned up the radio after ascertaining which number of the street she stayed on. Jack had no interest in whores, especially not junkie whores. He knew that some of the other drivers had regular clients who worked the streets and some even took sexual favours as payment but that wasn't for him. It wasn't that he looked down on them, he felt sorry for some of them, especially the ones who were working that life to feed a family not a heroin habit, but fuck getting involved with one of them, no chance! When Jack arrived at the drop off he eyed the mileage sheet and calculated the fare but he had done this run a few times anyway so was just double checking, 'That'll be £6:40 doll', he announced. No answer came from the back of the taxi and with no sign of movement he swivelled slowly in his seat to take in the scene. The girl sat was sat with her head right back breathing softly and at first Jack thought she had fallen asleep. 'Hey', he tried to snap her back to reality but then in horror he saw the needle sticking out of her forearm glinting in the streetlight they had pulled up alongside. 'Hey', Jack shouted this time mild panic beginning to envelop him. Surely to fuck this daft cow hadn't overdosed in the back of his fuckin cab? He leapt from the car and opened the back door and tried in vain to shake her awake. She was breathing he was sure but he noticed a speckle of white spittle frothing at the corner of her mouth. He remembered the number of the door she had requested and ran to it frantically rattling the letterbox. 'Aye awright, awright, where's the fuckin fire', came a male voice from inside. The cunt wouldn't open the door though till he knew who it was and what they wanted. So, breathlessly Jack had to explain from the other side of his urgent need for help. 'Fucks sake' said the voice on the other side. After what seemed like an age and numerous locks and chains had been undone, the door opened and out came a stocky figure dressed in a white tee shirt and jeans and sporting the same haunted look as his punter, the unmistakable trademark of another junkie fuck up. He followed Jack out to the car and none too carefully began to drag her out, 'fuck sake Kerry' he complained bitterly as he hauled her towards the house. Although concerned for her Jack couldn't help but feel relieved as the door slammed shut behind them with a 'sorry aboot this big man' as a farewell. Jack didn't even think about the fare he had just lost as he walked back to the car and then noticed her clutch bag lying on the backseat. He looked inside but there was fuck all in it apart from a few condoms and a few scraps of makeup, she probably had her cash tucked away somewhere more secure Jack reckoned. So, he left it at the door and then decided it was time to get out of dodge. He drove back to Phil Cotter's house in Halfway and posted his keys through the letterbox along with a hastily scribbled note.

Hi Phil,

Thanks for the job but I've decided this isn't for me so won't be doing any more shifts.

All the best, see you round,

Jack.

With that Jack jumped into his own car and headed for home looking forward to nuzzling in beside Rachel and her warm body. He'd had enough of this taxi driver lark and no mistake. He wondered what would be next. Surely couldn't be any fuckin worse he thought as he sped through the near empty streets.

The foundations of what did come next had been laid a few weeks earlier over a chat with Rachel's brother in law over a family dinner at Rachel's Mum's house. Paul Delaney was on rare visit home from London with Rachel's sister Emma when he heard about Jack's struggles to find work. He told Jack that in his capacity as an assistant manager of a demolition firm he could easily get him a few weeks work on one of his contracts and that he would be happy to put him up for the duration. For about forty quid a day Paul said he could get Jack a job labouring at one of the sites or if he could work a burner's torch or drive a forklift he could get him a bit more. 'Just give me a call if you decide to come down', Paul had said. Keen to keep all his options open Jack assured him he could do both. It had been a while but Jack had used both skills in the 'Craig, the burning whilst doing his ironworks training and the forklift semi regularly in the furnace. The minute Jack had put the keys of the Sierra Sapphire through Phil Cotter's letterbox Jack had decided to make that call and pretty soon afterwards he was off to London.

The contract was for six weeks to demolish what had been an old community hall and it was Jack's job to burn the bolts off the girders of the structure holding the building together. Then he would cut through the angles of the frame further weakening the structure allowing the digger machine to smash through the rest of it and tear the building apart. It had to be done section by section, making sure that the structure was safe to work within. Some of the work was at a height and Jack was a little nervous going up the ladder with his burning gear in tow but having worked in the 'Craig the rest of it came easily enough to him. Once a section was down the labourers would sift through the debris separating the rubble from the metal, retaining the sections of girder for Jack to cut into more manageable sizes and removing the precious metals like copper and lead which would be retained and sold in bulk to a scrap metal dealer. By way of a bonus all the lads on the job would get a share of the final scrap value when the project was complete.

On a nice day the work wasn't too unpleasant but when it was cold and the rain came they would retreat to the porta-cabin that was their base. Jack struggled to take to his cockney workmates and their fondness of calling him Jock even though he had told them umpteen times his name was Jack. It was a constant source of annoyance to him even though no real harm was meant by it. After a few days trying in vain to get to know them better and trying to make himself understood Jack pretty much gave up and retreated into himself just as he had done in the early days at the college. Relief came in the evenings in long telephone conversations with Rachel and the easy chat with Paul and Emma. Jack was discovering what being homesick felt like for the first time and it came as no small relief when Paul informed him that the project was ahead of schedule and if the weather held out they would likely be finished in four weeks instead of the six that had been bargained for. Although he had spent a few quid on a couple of afternoons out with Paul, Jack had lived pretty frugally what with Paul and Emma steadfastly refusing any money from him and with the bonus they would get for the scrap he would likely get home and up the road with around £1200. Not bad for a few weeks work. On his last day a few of the lads on the site arranged to take Jack out for a few pints and he was surprised to find that he was quite well thought of amongst them, maybe he'd misjudged them, although the language barrier still existed as they struggled to understand his broad Scottish drawl even more so after a few drinks. The next day Jack bought Emma the biggest bouquet of flowers he could find at the florists and Paul a bottle of the single malt he liked, then after they said their fond farewells Jack was away on the train back up to Scotland, back home, back to Rachel.

After falling into Rachel's arms at the train station the pair spent much of the next two days in bed making up for lost time, so it was Monday night before Jack began sorting through the mountain of mail waiting for him. Rachel had dealt with anything that looked like it needed immediate attention but in amongst the pile was a reply to a long forgotten application for a ticket conductor's job on the trains with Scotrail. Jack had been invited to sit an aptitude test at the companies training centre the following week. What a great weekend he thought to himself. He'd come home the conquering hero with a few quid in his tail and now there was another prospect on the horizon, things were looking up!

'Sometimes you're better being lucky than good' was one of the Chief's regular sayings and Jack was about to discover just what he meant by that. As the Scotrail hopefuls filtered through the lobby of the training centre just off Central station Jack eyed up the competition. Ahead there was a lady barking instructions but Jack wasn't paying much attention as he marvelled at the get up on some of his fellow applicants. Most were dressed smart but casual like Jack but some of these twats had a full suit and tie combo on for a fuckin test! 'Morons' Jack muttered to himself as he followed the crowd into the training room to his right. There was another to the left but Jack figured that there were so many applicants they needed both. They were told to find a seat where they could and Jack chose one in the middle halfway down the room. A tall skinny lad was handing out papers and smiled at Jack as he placed his in front of him and Jack had to the resist the urge to sneak a peek at the contents paying heed to the 'DO NOT TURN OVER UNTIL INSTRUCTED' warning on the front cover. Once everyone was settled down the skinny lad introduced himself as Graeme the personnel officer and ran through the instructions. They should fill out all their details on the cover sheet including their full address and postcode. There would be forty questions, they should take their time and once they had completed the test they were allowed to leave placing their paper on his desk taking care not to disturb those who were still working. There was one hour allotted to the test and all work would have to be handed in at the end of it, no extensions. With that it was time to turn over and begin.

Jack was surprised at some of the technical data in the questions for a conductor's job but given his background he didn't find it too difficult although challenging in parts and he breezed through around half the paper when he allowed himself a brief break. Puzzled at its content he turned to the front cover and stared in horror at the bold print in front of him.

APTITUDE TEST FOR TRAIN DRIVING OPERATIVE.

He glanced across at the other room and realised at once he was in the wrong place and the conductor's test must be across in the other room. Jesus wept, he'd fucked this up big time! He thought about bolting to the front and explaining his mistake but it was too late for that. There was nothing else for it he would just need to see this out and see what happened, after all he was absolutely skating this test. He couldn't possibly scam this could he? He carried on with the rest of the test brushing aside the worry over whether he'd fucked up an opportunity here. In no time at all he completed the work but all around still seemed to be beavering away, so he proof read his answers, something he'd always been scolded for not doing at school. Sure enough he found a couple of mistakes and rectified them. There was one puzzle with triangles he kept getting different answers for but he persevered with it and eventually settled on an answer he was happy with. Then, when was happy he wasn't going to be the first one to hand in his paper he made for the front and bolted for freedom, half expecting to be called back on the way out for not being on some list or other. No call came however and Jack was left to wonder how this might transpire.

The answer came just over a week later when he received a phone call from the Scotrail personnel office. Apparently he had skooshed the test and they wanted him to come in for an interview but there was a problem, they couldn't seem to find his application form in their system. Jack debated on the other end of the line whether to say they must have lost it or come clean. Honesty is always the best policy, Jack was reminded of another of the Chiefs sayings but on a whim he dismissed that notion. After all he had brassed it along thus far. Telling the truth would surely bring the curtain down on this episode. Instead he perpetuated the lie and waited for the response. 'Well, no problem we'll just get you to fill out another one. I'll send it through to you in the post along with the offer of interview and you can just bring it with you on the day.' Yassss!' He was in and the chance of a great job was still in the pipeline. Redemption was at hand and he wasn't about to let it slip away. Over the next few days he spoke to everyone he knew with any connection to Scotrail and amassed every bit of information he would need for the interview and he adapted his application form as necessary. His homework paid off and despite terrible nerves on the day he answered every question eloquently and confidently. A few weeks later he and Rachel were partying like rock stars as they celebrated his job offer with a rare night out in Glasgow, eventually falling into bed at 4 a.m. laughing and chatting excitedly about the future. Finally Jack had unlocked the door to a new beginning and not just with any job, a job that offered good terms and conditions and a salary of double nearly anything he'd been looking at! He couldn't quite believe his good fortune and couldn't wait to get started.

A few months after Jack began his training period with Scotrail, Jack and Rachel had that conversation that most couples have at some time or other as they debated when to start a family. Jack wanted to enjoy life but he was deeply aware of Rachel's yearning for motherhood and wasn't against the idea of cementing their relationship by bringing a new life into the world together. So, it was that they agreed she would come off the pill and they would try for a baby when Jack's training period was complete and he was safely ensconced in the job full time. Jack still had mild anxiety that some eagle eyed clerk would stumble upon his stroke of luck and cry foul at any minute.

It was to be as chastening an experience as any Jack had lived through the day he sat in the ultrasound room with Rachel lying on the bed ready for her first scan. The midwife was swirling the probe around on Rachel's belly as everyone stared at the snowy screen in front of them. To Jack it just looked like the telly all those years ago when all the channels had shut down for the night and he couldn't make head nor fuckin tail of it. His senses were heightened immediately though as the midwife said 'Yeah they both look absolutely fine.' Rachel seemed oblivious as she smiled dreamily at the screen. 'Both? Whit do ye mean both?' Jack asked incredulously. 'Oh didn't you know it was twins' asked a somewhat surprised midwife. 'Does this look like a fuckin face that knew?' was all that Jack could muster as Rachel continued to look absolutely oblivious. Fuck thought Jack. Two babies! Suddenly the two bedroom houses they'd been looking at seemed hopelessly inadequate. They'd have to rethink everything but at least they both had good jobs, Rachel in the court and Jack on the trains. They'd be alright wouldn't they? On the drive home they turned the notion over of what having twins would mean between each other. Frantically they discussed how they would cope and Rachel went from hysterical laughter to tears in a matter of seconds. Fuck! She's having a fuckin nervous breakdown right in front of me thought Jack. He stopped the car and they held on to one another until they both calmed down. Of course they'd cope with it, they'd deal with it no matter how scary because they had to and it'd all be alright but by fuck Jack Leonard was having to grow up quicker than he'd bargained for.

In the late summer of 1995 Rachel was busying herself in the kitchen, preparing the babies bottles as Jack came in to collect his sandwiches from the fridge for the shift ahead. 'Okay, I'm off now sweetheart', he told her as he kissed her deftly on the cheek not wanting to get in the way. 'Okay, see you tonight, have a good one,' Rachel chimed back. Jack turned and made for the living room where his baby girls Emma and Louise were babbling away excitedly to one another on their little bouncy chairs. They had named them both after Jack and Rachel's sisters. Jack paused to kiss them gently on the forehead as he smiled and said 'bye you little monkeys.' What a year it had been. A new job, a new house and an instant family to fill it with. They had faced it all together, Jack and Rachel, and come through the other side. Life was good thought Jack, as he headed for the train station and another shift on the Motherwell/Dalmuir line. His mind wandered back to the good old days in the 'Craig and his wee pal Ricky. Ricky and Gerry Bonner were the only ones Jack had really kept in touch with since the closure and come to think of it hadn't it been nearly two years since he'd last seen Ricky? He made a mental note to get him out for a pint soon and wondered if he was still going to the Rangers games. Jack still made it to the odd game at Parkhead when he could, but it was a tough slog these days with Rangers big spending sweeping all before them. One day their big spending would come back to haunt them and the tables would turn but Jack wasn't to know that and meantime had to make do with the odd moment in the sun, an old firm victory or a rare cup win. Jack wondered what lay in store for him today. 'Aaah well, whits fur ye'll no go by ye'. Jack smiled at the memory of the well-worn catch phrase from the furnace.

TOMMY AND ANGELA WILSON

There weren't many in the 'Craig who had a plan in place or a safety net for when the curtain inevitably came down on steel production in the big plant, but Tommy Wilson did. Tommy's brother James had been working down in Stoke-on-Trent for a number of years and had risen to management level in a long established firm specialising in the production of machined steel castings. The two brothers had often spoken of how Tommy and the family might move down there when the axe was finally wielded over the 'Craig. A plan was set in place. Tommy would take the years make up money and sign on for an engineering course that would enhance his skillset and make him an asset to the firm, for whilst some of his skills and experience from the furnace were transferable there were gaps to be filled. The two businesses, although on the face of it broadly similar had marked differences and Tommy was keen to make the transition as smooth as possible. Once Tommy had completed the course the family would move down lock, stock and barrel and James would ensure there would be a suitable post waiting for his brother. Tommy and Angela had been down many times, even staying over Christmas and New Year and it helped that Angela got on so well with James' wife Danielle and that the couple had two kids just a year older than their two, Amy and Tommy junior. They had looked at houses in the area and schools for the kids and with James and Danielle's inside knowledge it seemed as though the future was all mapped out for them. It was a great comfort to Tommy to know that a viable option was just waiting for him and the family whilst all around him in the furnace were confronted by uncertainty and fear of what the future might hold.

There was just one fly in the ointment, something was wrong. Tommy couldn't quite put his finger on what, but something was most definitely up with Angela and had been for some time. Although Angela had always been enthusiastic about the planned move to Stoke, lately she'd seemed reluctant to even discuss it. Where before there had been excitable chatter about the red brick houses with their pretty manicured lawns and edges filled with colourful blooms and animated discussions over which schools would best suit the kids, there was now an almost disinterested compliance with whatever Tommy had suggested. Tommy had long become used to Angela's mood swings, she suffered terribly from PMT at times but this was more than that and Tommy wasn't entirely sure he wanted to know what was at the root of it.

In the couple of years leading up to the closure Tommy had felt the distance between them grow. There had been a halcyon period for a few months when she was all over him or so it seemed, but it didn't last and round about the time of the snub over Davie Kellacher's wedding it seemed as though the darkness had descended on her again and he could feel that distance between them once more. Of course he had tried to talk to her about it. He had been stung by her response when he had suggested that she might be suffering from some form of depression, maybe even a late onset of post-natal depression even though the kids were long since up and away to school. 'You ever fuckin think it might be you that's the problem?' she had bitten back bitterly. Of course she apologised later and attempted to soothe his worries but something deep rooted was at work here and Tommy knew it. Although he was a trusting person, the type who always wanted to think the best of others, Tommy was in no way shape or form naïve. He knew that given Angela's behaviour it was conceivable that she could be having some sort of affair. He wasn't blind to the effect her curves and big brown, come to bed eyes and lashes had on other men. He just wasn't the jealous or possessive type, but all the same he couldn't ignore the signs and she had taken to going out a fair bit more with her friends of late and more often than not they were friends of whom Tommy knew little. So it was with great shame and a good deal of trepidation that for a time at least, that Tommy had taken to checking her purse or bag for some tell-tale sign, even checking her discarded underwear after nights out for some signs of sexual activity. He found nothing, apart from one Friday night when she came home particularly late and drunk. She had fallen asleep on top of the bed and Tommy took the opportunity to check her underwear again. It was wet and stained and when the morning sun began to creep its way into the room a few hours later Tommy thought he could see what looked like the beginnings of a bite mark on her shoulder. Of course Angela explained it all away in the morning. She'd had a discharge, an infection and was going to have to see the doctor and she'd bumped into something drunk last night, the mark was a bruise and what the fuck was he doing scanning her underwear? Why was he checking up on her? It had sparked a huge row between them and Tommy had ended up apologising, feeling her anger at him and accepting her explanation. It did nothing to calm the unease he felt though or that strange sinking feeling despite her apparent innocence and the distance between them remained.

After the showdown with Davie Kellacher in the café in Hamilton, Angela had been left bereft. She broke down on the spot and had poured her heart out to a complete stranger at the table opposite. 'He's not worth it hen, none of them are,' the kindly woman had told her. Oddly it had made her feel a little better and in Tommy she knew she had someone who was worth it and she resolved to try and make it work, but there was an ache in her heart where the fantasy of what a life with Davie Kellacher would look like used to reside. It was a fantasy though, she knew that. She had seen him first hand flirting away at the bar when they'd slipped out together for the evening. Talking to women came easily to Davie and he was tactile with them as well, putting them at ease and then making them laugh with some witty innuendo, disarming their scepticism with his smile and his charm. She'd flipped one night in the Popinjay Hotel down the Clyde valley. It should have been a romantic escape for them but there he was, charming the knickers off some posh blond totty at the bar. She'd had a real go at him when he came back over to their table and only the notion that he'd end up fucking said posh blond had kept her there as she considered storming out. Davie had darkened under her verbal assault and made it clear he found her jealousy unattractive. Angela made a mental note to keep her green streak under control but she knew there were others when she wasn't around. Yes, it was a fantasy no doubt, but some fantasies come true don't they?

For a time Angela threw herself into her family life at home, devoting herself to Tommy, partly in a bid to stop herself spiralling out of control and partly due to the enormous burden of guilt she felt toward her seemingly oblivious husband and of course there were the kids. They didn't deserve any of this. Old wounds sometimes open easily again though and when Tommy came home one night complaining of his surprise at not even meriting a night time invitation to the Kellacher-Angelis wedding of the year, Angela felt a wave of dread, hurt and regret envelop and consume her. Pretty soon she was again in the depths of despair and began moping around once more much to Tommy's distress. Redemption was to come a few months later when Angela listened open mouthed as Tommy told of how Davie Kellacher's dream marriage to Lucy Angelis was over and moreover after incurring the wrath of Billy Angelis, Davie was in hospital nursing some less than insignificant injuries. Angela's head was swimming with all of it but as soon as she heard that Davie would be in hospital for some time she knew that she simply had to see him. She needed closure, she knew that. She'd seen enough Trisha Goddard and Jerry Springer shows with people pouring their hearts out for the camera to know that that was exactly what she needed, even if a small part of her hoped that he might want to cling to her again in his hour of need. When she felt it was the safest time to visit, Angela donned her best makeup and a flattering outfit, although not so sexy as to raise eyes for a hospital visit or stir any suspicion in Tommy. When she saw him, she was surprised at how it made her feel. It was almost as if she was at last seeing him as he really was for the first time. She felt only pity and a sadness for him that it had come to this. As they locked eyes, Davie guessed wrongly that upon hearing of his split with Lucy that Angela had come to rekindle their affair. 'I'm no good Angela, I never will be. I fuck everything up and everyone around me suffers. I deserve this, but you don't, you deserve to be happy,' Davie said breathlessly. As if reading his thoughts Angela quietened him. 'Shush', she replied stroking his face softly. 'I've only come to see how you are.' For a few minutes they spoke over how Davie had gotten himself into this mess and boy was it a mess. Angela found herself feeling some sympathy with her nemesis Lucy and guessed that the poor girl must have been broken by what she been through and the horrors she must have witnessed at Davie's ill-fated house party. She smiled at Davie. 'We had some good times together didn't we?' she added. Before Davie could answer she bent over him and squeezed his hand gently before kissing him on the forehead. 'Goodbye Davie, I hope you find what you're looking for' she said and walked from the ward, her head held high.

It was with a sense of relief that Angela heard some time later that instead of attending the night shift at no 1 furnace, Davie Kellacher had in fact taken the night bus to London and was not expected back. A smart move thought Angela, after all, not too many get to cross the Angelis clan and live to tell the tale. Many times Davie had told her of his affection for old London town, it's cosmopolitan feel and multi-cultural vibe where no one gave a fuck whether you were Catholic, Protestant, Jewish or whatever. She knew that she would never see him again now, it was finally over and she had her closure and she hoped he would find happiness there somehow. Many times during their affair she'd had to bite back the urge to confess all to Tommy when the fantasy was at its height. Then thereafter as the guilt gnawed at her she was almost consumed by the need to give the pleading in Tommy's eyes the explanation they were so desperate for, but it was pointless now and would only hurt Tommy and do more harm than good she told herself. So Tommy took the engineering course and the years make up money and all the while the couple made preparations for the big move down to Stoke and Angela embraced it all fully, relishing the prospect of starting afresh. Ambitiously they bought in at the higher end of the housing market and as interest rates began to climb Angela was forced into taking on a job at the local snooker club. Rumours are doing the rounds that she is fucking the manager there, but Tommy

Wilson, family man and all round good guy, remains blissfully oblivious.

THE CHIEF AND DAVIE KELLACHER

If British Steel had made good on their promise of keeping the plant open until at least 1994 the chances are that the Chief need not have worked another day in his life. Typically though they reneged sending the whole of Lanarkshire into meltdown and throwing the Chief's retirement plans out the window. So, the big fella somewhat reluctantly was thrust like the others onto the employment market. His salvation was to come in the form of an old long since forgotten PSV licence tucked away in the drawer of his bedside cabinet. The Chief had driven the buses years ago before entering the 'Craig, working for local firms like Cotters and Stuart's amongst others. He did the football supporter runs, pilgrimage to Parkhead one weekend, homage to Ibrox the next. He did the pensioner day trips to Largs and Ayr and occasionally down to the Lake District. The work though was sporadic and dependant on bookings and unless you were with a big firm conditions weren't great and anyway the longer runs played havoc with his sciatica. The Chief's Dad Roy had worked in the steel industry man and boy. First the Clyde Alloy then Stewart and Lloyds before ending up a crane driver down at the finishing end in the 'Craig. When his father produced a form for jobs in the blast furnace there was no decision to be made and the Chief was soon joining his Dad at the Craigneuk time clock of a morning. The big man soon made his way through the ranks there as well with his aptitude, time keeping and hard work ethic coming to the fore until eventually after a retirement he reached the top manual grade as the man in charge of the hot blast stoves. The hot blast stoves were huge, vertical cylindrical shells lined with firebrick. They took in and recycled hot gasses from the furnace and coke ovens to provide a hot blast that allowed the smelting process to reach fantastic temperatures of up to 1600 degrees. Obviously such a heady mix of gases and high temperatures had its dangers and it was a responsible job managing the process. The Chief though, was a bright well-read and well educated man, easily equipped for it even though his study had stopped with the eleven plus exam at school, as coming from a poor background another wage was needed. The Chief had been sounded out a few times about making the step up to management as well but that was a step too far for him, after all there was enough stress at times in his own job. No, management was a young man's game the Chief had decided and though there was plenty of talent amongst them there were also enough fools on that side of things to make it doubly unattractive.

That emphasis on being a provider had never left him and he wasn't about to let the side down now. Although he could have comfortably sat and lived off the redundancy for a while and waited it out till retirement he and his wife Margaret had plans. They had a stack of old VHS videos of all the cruise ships you could take from all over the world and they watched them regularly marvelling at the sights you could see. They had been on a couple across the Med and the Adriatic but they wanted to do more and there was talk of getting one of those VW camper vans and touring Scotland and the rest of Europe. Then there were the Grandkids. Scott and Emily were growing fast and would be starting school soon. The Chief and Margaret wanted to play a full part in their lives, be able to treat them and help the kids out as well as they made their way in the world. Then there was the garden. The Chief took great pride in his garden and had spent many a long hour out there cultivating and planting to turn it into one of the most alluring in the area. People would often stop and look at it as they passed by and if they did and he happened to be out there working at the time, he would pass the time of day with them, always happy, especially to pass on any tips on new blooms or looking after the lawn. It was an impressive sight with the perfectly manicured sloping lawn at the front, routinely adorned by strategically placed shrubs and flowers, their colours designed to complement one another. At the side of the house sat his big Nissan Bluebird, the family car of choice for a generation, no room for it in the adjoining garage such were the number of gardening tools and aids the chief had stocked in there. Along the path at the side of the house there was an archway of ivy over the top of the entrance gate to the back door, a sort of special passageway to the secret garden that was designed so that the grandkids could make the best use of it in summer. There was a large strip of rectangular lawn, perfectly edged and adorned with all sorts of colourful characters such as woodland animals and gnomes and the even the odd Disney character. At the back of the garden and tucked away in the corner away from the potential harm of the kids ball games stood his well-stocked greenhouse for the tomatoes and his bedding plants which he often gave away to friends and family when they were ready. In front of that there was a little planting area for the rhubarb and the lettuce cordoned off from the rest to keep it safe from predators and rampaging grandchildren. All in all it was quite the sight around Coltness, but it was a lot of work and for now at least it would have to wait along with the cruises and the plans for camper vans and the rest. The Chief had a couple of years graft to do yet to fund the sort of retirement he and Margaret had promised each other.

So, the Chief began calling old friends, calling in favours to see what he could shake loose from the employment jungle tree. Pretty soon he had an in with the SMT buses courtesy of his old pal Ronnie Whyte from the Market Bar and his name was put forward for a vacancy on one of the routes. Within a short time the Chief would become a familiar face on the 240 route from Wishaw to Glasgow passing through familiar territory like Motherwell, Bellshill and Viewpark. His big booming voice and cheery disposition soon made him a favourite amongst the punters. If the Chief had a failing it was that he was an incurable gossip but even that proved to be an asset in this job and he soon became a conspiratorial confidant amongst the old wifeys and daytrippers heading into town. Of course on such a route there would be the occasional problem with some pale faced, anorexic junkie trying to get wide or some drunk refusing to pay or causing a stir on the night bus home. The Chief was plenty fit for any of that though with his big booming voice and strapping frame warning enough for most and failing that he had a fine line in the banter able to diffuse most situations. He was so popular amongst the pensioner crowd that more than one of them nominated him for a community service award to the council and he was invited along to a lavish ceremony in the banquet hall at the County Buildings in Hamilton. He didn't win but he still considered it an honour to have been nominated. So it was with no little regret that his manager at the SMT had to send out his letter advising him of his impending retirement date when the time came. There were no regrets for the Chief though. He'd enjoyed his time on the buses but it was time to get busy living that life that he and Margaret had envisaged for themselves.

The Chief's daughter Fiona and her husband Mark were approaching an important anniversary and Mark wanted to take her away for a romantic weekend in Rome. Of course he and Margaret were happy to have the kids for the weekend but the Chief figured it wasn't fair for the kids to miss out on a wee holiday. Could they take the kids down to London the same weekend? After some initial reticence from Fiona they agreed and the Chief began making plans. A nice hotel in Bayswater was booked and the Chief set about making an itinerary, they would do all the sights, well as many as time constraints would allow. Margaret loved to see her husband like this, doing all his regimental planning and organisation for a trip away and she left him to it. 'He'll have the legs walked off the poor kids by the end of the weekend' Margaret laughed to herself. There would be a wee boat trip down the Thames, a visit to HMS Belfast, the houses of Parliament and 10 Downing Street. They'd visit the Natural History Museum and Madam Tussaud's, Buckingham Palace and if the weather held Hyde Park. He'd even leave a little time for some shopping on Oxford Street, a visit to Hamleys the big toy store for the kids and the world famous Harrods for Margaret. Over the course of the next few weeks the Chief busied himself studying train timetables and underground maps and booking attraction tickets. All they needed was a bit of luck with the weather and it would be perfect. The Chief wanted things to go like clockwork after all his daughter was entrusting him and Margaret with her most precious cargo. This was their first holiday away with the Grandkids without Fiona and Mark and the Chief didn't want it to be the last, there was so much he wanted to help teach them about the world at large and help give them a great start in life.

Davie Kellacher was shaking off a heavy one, the smell of stale drink and dope hanging heavy on his breath as he waited for the tube to rattle into the station. He was running late again and he'd already had one warning about his timekeeping. He couldn't afford to fuck this job up like he'd royally fucked up the last one. It had been a good job too, re-routeing the line at Watford junction with the maintenance crew, good money as well. How was he supposed to have known that the redhead with that shapely arse he found so hard to resist was in fact the shift foreman's daughter, not just any shift foreman either. George O'Mara was a great clunking mass of Dublin menace standing at 6 feet 4 inches tall and built like a fuckin garden shed. It wasn't as if Davie had gone chasing it either, as far as he could remember the redhead who looked a bit like the lead singer from Tpau, (what was her name again?) had put it on a fuckin plate for him. He knew he was in trouble on the Sunday night when he was told who she was and when some of the lads on the shift who had been in the pub that night started gossiping about it and winking at him conspiratorially at work next day, he knew he was on borrowed time. The call came that Monday night. George had found out and the big Irishman was gunning for Davie and was asking around for his address. George O'Mara was not a man to be trifled with, there were rumours he'd been an active member of the Provos, but whether true or not Davie had seen him lift fuckin railway sleepers with his bare hands and he'd heard the story of how it took 6 coppers to lift him after he had gotten a bit carried away with a rare Irish victory over England at the rugby. He wasn't hanging around to try and reason with him. He'd already had his face rearranged once over a fathers love for his daughter and he had no desire to go through that again. So, he packed up his things and took the tube across the city and bunked in with a mate in a flat in Bethnal Green, cursing himself for having written off another good thing in pursuit of fanny.

They used to say the streets of London were paved with gold, well not in Davie's experience they weren't. It had taken him a good bit longer than he'd hoped to get sorted with another job but his new flat mate had come to the rescue with a labouring job at a site on the fringes of Soho. It was a complete tear down and re-build job that would provide work for at least a year. Davie loved London. There were all the colours of the rainbow to choose from here, black, brown, yellow or white. Chinese, Japanese, Aussie or American tourists he didn't give a fuck, he'd shagged them all. It was a sort of United Nations of fanny and Davie was happy enough to take a tour of the globe. Just last week he'd fucked a Spanish school teacher on a trip with her primary school. He'd noticed her at the bar, the material of her denim skirt straining against the weight of her shapely arse. He moved in for the kill as the tequilas her and her friends had been downing began to take their toll and pretty soon he was fucking her up an alley round the back of the pub. Fuck, he hadn't done that for years, his bare arse blowing in the wind, his trousers round his ankles as he took her up against the wall. He'd even bagged himself a fuck buddy with no strings attached for when pickings were slim. Petra was a German girl in her mid-twenties and was nanny to a wealthy family in the Chelsea area. She'd met Davie at a house party in Fulham and they'd bonded over a shared love of the weed. It transpired that the family Petra worked for scheduled Monday and Thursday as evenings to spend quality time with their kids so her services weren't required on these nights. Who the fuck does that? Write their weans into some kind of fuckin schedule? Anyway, as Petra's friends were often busy on these nights she was on occasion at a loose end and Davie knew just how to fill her time. So, semi regularly they would meet up at his for a fuck, occasionally going out for a drink or staying in for a smoke afterwards. Davie saw it as refreshing and honest and no feelings were involved, just two lonely people passing their time together and satisfying a need within themselves. There was no joy in much of any of it for Davie these days, it was just an itch that had to be scratched.

Last night had been a typical Davie fuck up. It was getting close to the anniversary of his sweet Mum Anna's passing and he'd decided to have a few drinks at his local the Earl Grey, just to take the edge off his melancholy. Ironically after a just a few pints and a couple of whiskies Davie began to get maudlin over Anna and his lost love Lucy Angelis. The 'Craig had been closed down for a while and Davie well settled in to his new life in London when word came from Scotland that Anna had contracted lung cancer. A few months later and further word came that she wasn't doing well and was in hospital with the prognosis not looking good. Davie decided he had to see her. It was a risk as Davie had been told that Billy Angelis had been looking for him and was offering a reward for info on his whereabouts, but it was a risk he felt he had to take. After being reassured by his old pal Gus that Angelis was unaware as yet that Anna was in hospital, Davie made plans to head for Scotland and took the last train stealing into Motherwell in the dead of night. When Anna laid eyes on her precious son for the first time in over three years she nearly hyper-ventilated. 'It's too dangerous son, Angelis still hot for you, won't give it up' she whispered breathlessly pulling the oxygen mask from her face. Davie looked at her sadly, she was just a bag of bones lying there waiting to pass on to the other side as she called it. Davie calmed and soothed her, stroking her face as he promised to take the next train back and all the time lying to her about the wonderful life he was leading in the big smoke.

Davie was as good as his word and headed back to London on the next train having promised Anna he wouldn't return unless he had assurances his safety would be guaranteed. Just four weeks later the phone call Davie had been dreading came to tell him that Anna had passed away during the night. Davie charged his old friend Gus with making enquiries as to whether it would be safe for him to return and attend her funeral, hoping against hope that Angelis might find some compassion from somewhere for him at this terrible time. When word came back it wasn't what Davie had hoped for. Angelis made it clear that if he was to set foot anywhere near Anna's funeral he would make sure the job he'd started on Kellacher the day after he had ruined his daughter's life was finished off once and for all. Davie hoped that this was the final insult from Angelis but it didn't really matter. He would never return home now, there was nothing left there for him now. In the run up to the funeral and normally fuelled by a few drinks Davie considered risking all and defying the warnings from Angelis to say his farewells to Anna. He even got as far as Victoria station one night as he considered taking night bus up to Scotland, but the instinct of self-preservation and the memory of his last promise to Anna always got the better of him. The day of the funeral Davie went to the Earl Grey alone and drank pints of Guinness washed down with gin chasers, Anna's tipple of choice, the old mothers ruin. When he was spent he staggered home crying silent tears in the rain. Almost a year on from that night and here he was again drowning his considerable sorrows when the entrance of a noisy group of Jamaicans shook him from his self-indulgence.

Keith, the landlord of the Earl Grey grimaced as he inhaled the unmistakable whiff of the ganja emanating from the group in the corner. If the pub had been busy or it had been a Friday or Saturday night he might have told them to sling their hook, but as it was it had been a quiet Sunday and he'd only had a few regulars in and that miserable looking fuckin Jock in the corner. 'What the fuck is his problem' wondered Keith? Aaah well at least he's spending a bit of money at the bar he thought as he tried to make a quick mental calculation of how many pints and shorts the miserable cunt had drunk. Pretty soon though he was engulfed by the Jamaicans at the bar as they ordered cans of Red Stripe and rums and bacardis. They were noisy as fuck and Keith reckoned they were all as high as fuckin kites but he'd had them in the pub a few times and they'd never been any bother.

Davie was fascinated by the colourful crowd opposite him and as usual his eyes were drawn to the women in the company. One of them smiled at him and called over, 'You look like ya got the weight o' the world on them shoulders boy. Why don' ya turn that frown upside down and come an' join us eh?' It was an invitation Davie wasn't about to turn down and pretty soon he was putting the world to rights with the girl in question who happened to be called Anique and her boyfriend Elijah. Elijah was a strapping lad of around 6 foot 3, dreadlocks down to his shoulders and Davie guessed that his easy going demeanour hid a more aggressive side that could easily be unlocked when challenged. The pair of them bonded over stories of police prejudice toward their respective communities although in truth Davie was just recycling old stories he'd heard from the travelling community and he'd experienced little of what Elijah was talking about. Still, he wasn't to know that and it gave him a way in with the group and the increasingly tactile and flirtacious Anique.

After a couple of hours Elijah noticed the ever more hostile glares coming from Keith on the other side of the bar and figuring that the now overpowering stench of the ganja was getting under his skin he decided to call time on their session in the pub. At his insistence the group began to drink up, they would take the party back to Elijah's now. 'Fuck me, a house party now', thought Davie. This Sunday night had taken an interesting turn for the better and he discarded any thoughts of what Monday morning at the site might look like after this. 'Whit's fur ye'll no go by ye', the saying flashed momentarily through Davie's mind. Back at the house Davie noticed that Elijah had a guitar propped up against the wall in the lounge. His head was swimming now as the copious amounts of whisky and Guinness he'd consumed took their toll and not only that he'd topped it up with some rums and the reefer that had been passed around in the pub. For a moment as the fresh air hit him on the short walk to Elijah's flat Davie thought he might throw up but he composed himself and the sight of the guitar had refocussed his mind. Playing always made him feel better and he asked Elijah's permission to use his guitar. Elijah looked at him with surprise etched upon his face. 'You play man? Yeah be my guest'. There was more to this Scotsman than met the eye he considered.

Always know your audience. It was one of the few things his father had drummed into Davie when he was a kid before he had fucked off to the bright lights. Davie hadn't really understood what it meant until he got a lot older, but he understood now and he understood what it would mean tonight. So, of course some Bob Marley tunes got an airing but he surprised and charmed his audience in equal measure by mixing it up a bit and throwing in a bit of Peter Tosh, Maxi Priest and then some Aswad and even a little of UB40. Elijah and even better Anique were suitably impressed but all too soon it seemed that people were beginning to drift away and the party was coming to an end. Davie hung back in the kitchen reluctant to contemplate any thoughts of the shift tomorrow. Anique came over to him. 'Ya played great, ya got some real talent there boy,' she said and then she kissed him. Gently at first and then, holding her lips on him until he responded, more urgently, her tongue darting in and out of his mouth. Davie was vaguely aware of the lurking figure of Elijah, standing in the kitchen doorway, laughing silently at the scene before him. A few minutes later the three of them fell into bed together with the boys either side of Anique. They didn't have sex though, they were all way too wasted for that. A couple of hours later Davie awoke in a panic and stole out quietly into the night. He felt sure he'd be seeing Elijah and Anique again though and soon.

None of all that mattered now though. All that counted was Davie being able to slip quietly onto site without his late arrival being noticed. He'd fallen into one of those micro sleeps at Tottenham Court Road and missed his stop, waking just as the doors closed. No matter though, he'd get off at Oxford Circus and cut through at the square, hopefully slipping quietly through the back end of the site and out of dodge. Davie felt the cold blast of air as the train pulled clear of the tube station and swallowed down some bile as the remnants of last night's booze and ganja cocktail threatened to make an early morning appearance. He turned his collar up against the following wind as he made his way up the steps to street level, then as he surveyed the morning throng of shoppers and tourists streaming towards him he caught sight of the unmistakable figure of the Chief ambling towards him with two little kiddies in tow. Instinctively, Davie put his head down and turned his collar up still further against the unseasonably chill wind. For a second he considered stopping and reminiscing with the big fella over the good old days in the 'Craig. How were young Jack and Ricky getting on? Did he still see wee Rab? Then he remembered the contempt the Chief had held him in after the whole Angela Wilson affair and dismissed the notion. Besides he was running late and he had no desire to unwittingly provide any leads for his nemesis Billy Angelis.

The Chief was having another productive morning in the capital. He'd left Margaret to have a lie in this morning whilst he took the kids to Hamleys, the big toy store, although in truth he was also trying to avoid packing for home which was a job always best avoided in his experience. Hamleys was a huge place and the Chief was glad he'd decided to make an early start. The kids were delighted with their purchases, Emily got the doll she'd been after and Scott was just about on the ceiling when the Chief agreed to buy him the Buzz Lightyear he was eyeing up. Now they were heading for the yellow MacDonald's sign in the distance for a bite to eat before heading back to the hotel for check out time. As the Chief eyed the crowd just exiting the underground station he recognised the familiar gait of one Davie Kellacher heading towards him. The mop of floppy, jet black hair swept to the side was showing signs of some grey flecks at the sides but there was no doubting it was him and the Chief felt sure that their eyes had locked albeit for just a split second. His natural curiosity was immediately aroused over where the boy had been and what had happened to him since he'd skipped town. Then he remembered the affair with Tommy's wife and that familiar distaste for the boy and his lifestyle flashed through his mind. It wasn't that he disliked him, it was more that he found what he had done unforgiveable and he considered the esteem in which the young lads, particularly Ricky and Jack had held him in as inappropriate. They were good young kids and they deserved better role models than this womanising, serial fuck up. It hadn't always been that way though and the Chief cast his mind back to the night Davie had held the whole of shift no 2 in the palm of his hand when they had pulled the nightshift at Hogmanay. He could picture Davie singing 'the Streets of London', eyes closed, lost in the music and not a care in the world, the rest of the boys transfixed. The Chief smiled at the memory.

Here he was now on the very streets of London, walking towards him and as Kellacher drew closer the Chief decided he would be polite and conciliatory if the boy stopped to speak to him. Let bygones be bygones. He wouldn't be carrying any tales back to Wishaw either. The Chief knew that Billy Angelis was still anxious to trace Davie Kellacher but filth like that could do their own dirty work, besides the boy was a 'Craigie' man and an ex colleague and the Chief's loyalties lay with him despite his failings. Christ, he might even give the lad a hug. He looked like he could do with one, the nick of him, he looked as a rough as a badgers and the Chief figured he'd been in some scrape or other last night as usual. The Chief kept his eyes fixed on the boy hoping for some scrap of recognition but Davie Kellacher turned his collar up against the world, kept his head down and walked on by...........

HARRY BADNEWS

Harry MacDonald or Harry Badnews as he had come to be known, had a Saturday ritual that he had stuck to religiously for a good few years since redundancy had forced him into a somewhat premature retirement. Up with the larks in the morning, never any later than 7, then into the bathroom for a quick sploonge before heading downstairs for a mug of black tea with 4 sugars. You didn't want to be hanging about in that bathroom anyway, fuckin freezing in there it was. The convector heater in it hadn't worked for years and Harry had never bothered his arse to get it fixed after she left. She was Alice McSevenny now, remarried to that slippery fucker Rab and living together as man and wife, bold as fuckin brass, just a few streets away from him. In truth, their paths didn't cross too often after all they didn't really move in the same circles. The happy couple were always off somewhere on some jaunt or other, trips into town to drink wine in some pretentious pub, wee runs down to the garden centre and nature trails down the Clyde Valley or weekends away down at the Lakes or up in the Highlands. The circumference of Harry's circle was by contrast much smaller and generally consisted of the tap shop, the bottom shop and the three bookies vying for punters business in the Main street. On the rare occasions they did come across one another in Overton, Harry would cross the street to the other side before he would give them the time of day and he guessed that arrangement suited them just fine such was the bitterness that remained between them.

After his tea Harry would get dressed and brave the elements rain, hail or shine. He would head down the street and into Curleys for the morning papers, some Morton's rolls and slices of square sausage. Back at home he would spread the papers out on the kitchen table, the Sporting Life for form and the Star for the tips. He would place his tobacco tin to the side always making sure he had four roll ups ready to spark up for a smoke, if not he would delve deftly into the tin of Golden Virginia and make up some more as he scanned the form guides for a hidden gem. He would cook up the square sausage and slap them onto the buttered crispy rolls before adding a sliver of brown sauce and all washed down with another mug of black tea with 4 sugars. After perusing the form guide in the Sporting Life Harry would turn on the television set for the Morning Line on Channel 4. Sometimes you could glean some extra snippets of info missed by the papers and of course they had the up to date info on the conditions, whether the going was good to soft or whatever. The only downside was the ramblings of that cunt McCririck on it and sure enough here he was shooting his big trap off and waving his arms about like a fuckin demented seagull. 'Hate that bastard', Harry muttered to himself as he refocussed on this afternoon's race card. Once Harry had scribbled out his bookies lines it was time to brace the elements again and head back out to place his bets. It was a process that could take some time as he debated laying on some of the tips rather than betting on his first instincts but he always tried to time it so that he was setting foot outside just as the pubs were opening up for the day. Then it was back down the street maybe popping into the tap shop for a half and a half pint along the way. Sometimes he would stay for a few and chat to some of the regulars or some of the young team who would be in for a few pints before heading down to Motherwell for the football. Occasionally he would even challenge the young ones to a game of pool catching up with whatever dramas they'd been involved in at that new big club that had opened in Hamilton, the Palais or Palace or whatever the fuck it was called. Lately though, Harry had become more insular, more often than not shunning the pub and just heading back to Curleys for a bottle of Whyte & McKay. It had been ages since he'd taken the bus over to Wishaw as well for his monthly trek to the Market Bar. Once a month and always on a Friday Harry had taken to heading there to meet up with wee Rab McLuckie and the Chief for a few drinks, a few bets and a reminisce about the good old days in the 'Craig. For a time Harry was fascinated by the busy lives both of this pair were leading in retirement. Wee Rab was always off somewhere or other, to the dogs at Shawfield with his boy or his nephew or a race meet at Hamilton. Then there were the Cotters or Shearings holidays with Sandra up to Oban or down to the Lakes or Blackpool. The Chief was just as busy since retiring from the buses it seemed. If he wasn't constructing some landscape wonder in the garden, it was the school run for the grandkids or he and Margaret were off on some far flung adventure. After a while the stories of their busy lives began to grate on Harry and in part at least were one of the reasons his monthly visits to the Market Bar came to a halt. These days Harry was happier with his own company.

Once Harry had made his selections for the day it was time to compare the odds that the various bookies had to offer. He would check in at Ladbrokes first, then along to Joe Coral's to see who was offering the best returns although there was rarely much of a difference. Occasionally he would go all the way along to the end of the street to the independent bookies Wilsons hoping catch a rare gem when maybe one of his picks for the day had drifted in on the betting but the independents hadn't picked up on it yet. Not today though, today he was sticking to his routine apart from one small detail. Instead of picking up the usual bottle of Whyte & MacKay at Curleys he would treat himself to a bottle of the single malt he liked so much. He'd had his eye on the bottle of Macallan's that Ali had in the locked display case behind the counter for a while and Harry decided that today was the day he would like to take it home with him.

'Special occasion Harry?' said Ali as he made his purchase. 'Aye, you could say that', said Harry in his standard one line reply. Ali always had some comment to make or other, usually inane chit chat about the weather with Harry grunting a yay or nay in response, never much more. They were a hard working lot the Pakistani's thought Harry, the shop was always open at 5.30 am on the dot every morning and never shut before 10 p.m. He'd heard some of the locals would complain about the smell in the shop at times but Harry thought his own house probably smelled worse. He had noticed it more since the wild winds of the winter had torn the whirligig outside to pieces and he'd had to start hanging his washing up inside, but he didn't give a fuck and besides there were never any visitors to comment on it these days. As Harry headed for home he thought about the preparations he had made for the future just the week before. He had been sparked into action after a conversation with the Chief in which he'd suggested that it wasn't out with the realms of possibility that his ex, Alice could be due some money from his estate in the event of his passing and could have some claim on his pension if he hadn't made a will. Harry couldn't remember the divorce settlement making any mention of this stuff, he'd just signed the papers and fucked off, keen to get away from the suits and back in amongst his own kind in the pub. For months he did nothing about it but it had gnawed away at him until finally he had made an appointment at Ness & Gallagher solicitors in Wishaw just in the last week. Now it was all sorted and he was sure she would get fuck all. He couldn't bear the thought of it, her dining out on his pension money with McSevenny. Fuck them and their fancy holidays and days out in the town at jazz clubs and the like. All the money would be split now such as it was between his son Graham and daughter Audrey. He hadn't seen Graham in over a year now. He'd moved away down south years ago to Leeds or was it Harrogate? Harry could never remember. He had a grandchild too but Harry had only seen the little mite twice. He got on alright with Graham and for a time the lad had visited regularly after the split with Alice but they had little to say to one another once Graham had got him up to speed with his life. Other than regaling his son of his monthly visit to the Market Bar and his latest failures with the bookie Harry didn't have much to add and he found himself regurgitating old stories from the past he'd told the boy a thousand times. When it came time to say goodbye it came as a relief to both of them and now, well, the boy just didn't come, he had his own life to lead and Harry understood that. Harry's relationship with his daughter was another matter. He didn't like the way she had taken her mother's side after the split, even ingratiating herself with McSevenny and Harry considered it a betrayal. All the same, when the time came, she'd get exactly the same as her brother, 50/50 split right down the middle. Fair's fuckin fair after all!

Harry opened the bottle of Macallan's and settled down in front of the television set flicking it into life with the remote control. The settee was old and worn now, almost threadbare in parts and Harry realised he should have replaced it years ago but he had no interest in furniture. He poured himself four fingers of the single malt and settled down to watch the afternoon's racing. 'Aaaaaah', Harry sighed as he enjoyed the warm glow from the single malt, feeling it burn gently as it slid down his throat. Then he set the glass down and reached for the tin of Golden Virginia. After sparking up another roll up Harry reached for the single malt again and sat back in satisfaction as he watched the smoke curl towards the artexed ceiling now yellowed by years of nicotine and neglect. One by one Harry watched his horses fail that afternoon, toasting each failure with a glass of Macallan's. When the last race ended he got unsteadily to his feet and scrunched the now redundant bookies lines into a ball and tossed them into the bin. Harry eyed the bottle of Macallan's on the table, there was enough there for one last drink he figured. He made his way across the living room staggering slightly before pausing in front of the old mahogany wall unit that housed the old record player and some records as well as a few ornaments and knick-knacks collected down the years. He rummaged around inside the cupboard of the unit for a few seconds before finding what he was looking for, an old dusty copy of the Perry Como song 'And I Love you So.' Yes, thought Harry, this occasion calls for some music, although it had been so long since he had played a record on the stereo he wasn't sure if the fucker would still work. Sure enough though, it crackled into life. The song had been the first dance at the silver wedding bash he'd thrown on a whim after a big win at the bookies way back in 1979. Harry smiled at the memory of gliding round the floor, Alice in his arms and him looking the part in the frilly shirt and bow tie and the dark brown suit he'd bought especially for the occasion. They'd been happy back then or so he thought, but all good things come to an end eventually and the faded pictures of that night were stuffed away in a drawer now, long since forgotten. No matter his bitterness towards her now he still loved the tune though. Harry drained the last of the Macallan's and made for the stairs singing along with Perry as he went.

Yes, I know how fuckin lonely life can be, Harry belted it out like he hadn't sung in years. Halfway up the stairs he paused and let rip with an enormous fart. He laughed to himself at the notion he might have followed through, but what did it matter now? Once at the top of the stairs, Harry made his way into the bathroom. He clambered unsteadily on to the side of the bath, almost falling at one point but managing to save himself by grabbing hold of the sink. He reached up for the light flex, long since bereft of a bulb and pulled it from the ceiling rose above. Then, after yanking on it to make sure it would hold, he tied it as tightly round his neck as he could stand and leapt to his death.

It took almost three weeks for Harry's body to be found and even then it was only because the workers on Mrs. Anderson's roof across the way had spotted the tell-tale shadow of Harry's legs swinging in the air through the frosted glass of the bathroom window. The boys in blue at the local cop shop had taken a bit of persuading to leave their mid-morning coffees and bacon rolls but eventually they were convinced to make their way over to Harry's and found him as the workmen had described. No one had any ideas as to why Harry did what he did and the only visible sign was perhaps in his visit to the solicitor's to tidy his affairs the week before. There was no note, nothing, only a Perry Como single on the record player and the television switched on and barely audible on channel 4 and an empty bottle of Macallan's on the kitchen table. One things for sure, as Harry breathed his last, he finally felt that knot in his stomach that had troubled him for so long, finally unravel and leave him be.

Rest in peace Harry!

The closure of Ravenscraig in 1992 signalled the end of large-scale steelmaking in Scotland and cost around 770 jobs within the plant itself, with another 10,000 job losses directly and indirectly attributed to the closure. The author James Lees worked within the blast-furnace from 1985 till its reduction to a one furnace operation in 1991.

Following on from its closure Ravenscraig left behind one the largest derelict sites in Europe measuring over 1,125 acres or put into context an area equating to 700 football pitches or twice the size of Monaco. (Source - Wikipedia)

The efforts to reclaim the land and rejuvenate the area continue to this day ....

Printed in Poland
by Amazon Fulfillment
Poland Sp. z o.o., Wrocław

60225514R00082